Deirdre Madden is from Toomebridge, Co. Antrim. Her novels include *The Birds of the Innocent Wood, Nothing is Black, One by One in the Darkness* (shortlisted for the Orange Prize) and *Molly Fox's Birthday* (also shortlisted for the Orange Prize). She teaches at Trinity College Dublin and is a member of the Irish arts academy Aosdána.

D0880300

DEIRDRE MADDEN

Remembering Light and Stone

faber and faber

First published in 1992
by Faber and Faber Limited
Bloomsbury House, 74–77 Great Russell Street
London WC1B 3DA

This Paperback edition first published in 1993

Phototypeset by Wilmaset Ltd, Wirral,

Printed and bound by CPI Group (UK) Ltd, Croydon, CR0 4YY
*A CIP record for this book is
available from the British Library*

ISBN 978–0–571–16946–7

4 6 8 10 9 7 5 2

for Harry, with love

'I don't belong here.' The thought came to me with such force that I almost said it aloud, at once, but I stopped myself just in time. I know what he would have said, reasonably: 'Do I?'

Later, looking back on that last day in Rome, what I would remember would be the heat and the noise. It was a struggle to be in the city because of that, but there was a curious softness too. The violent heat released the scent of fruit from the stalls as we walked past: melons, peaches, nectarines, plums. The fruit and vegetables were stacked outside the little shops in frail wooden crates. Near Campo Dei Fiori there was a woman who tended a stall, and she was singing as she brushed the city dust from the fruit with a spray of coloured feathers. It was the longest day of the year.

Ted wanted a drink, so we sat down at a table outside a café. We didn't say much to each other as we sat there, but watched the people drift along the hot street in their gaudy summer clothes and heavy jewellery. After a while Ted said to me that, for him, there was always a strong sense of death in the south, because of the very emphasis on life. The sun itself that made the fruit so ripe and big, that seemed to make the people bloom so early and so evidently, mercilessly pushed everything over into decay, so that the fruit quickly rotted, and the people suddenly fell into a graceless old age.

I thought of Franca's daughter, Lucia. She was fifteen, almost a woman and completely at ease with the fact, but I could see what Ted meant. I could see the short duration of that ease, and how there was something frail and uncertain about her whole self, as though she might at any moment topple headlong into being an old woman in a black dress, with nothing to look forward to but death. Time and again I remembered looking into the faces of young women in Italy, and seeing peer back, unbeknownst to them, the faces of the women they would be some fifty years later.

So I understood what Ted meant, and in a way I agreed with him, but I wasn't completely convinced, because I didn't want to be. I associated the north with violence and death, and I had come south to escape that.

Deep down, I knew that what he said was true, and that it was one of the many things people didn't understand about Italy, the people, that is, who came south to Italy, where 'everybody is so happy.' No one wants to shatter the myth of the warm, sensual, happy south, for if we did not believe in that, where would people go to escape the rigour of the north? I had learnt a lot about Italy in the time I had been there, but what I had learnt most of all was how little I understood it, how deceptive a country it was. And more than learning anything about Italy, I had found out more about my own country, simply by not being in it. The contrast with Italy was a help, but in many ways I felt I could have gone anywhere, so long as it was far away and provided me with privacy, so that I could forget all about home for a while, forget all about Ireland, and then remember it, undisturbed.

Once, I visited some limestone caverns up near Trieste, and it reminded me of the Burren, where I grew up. I realized then how much I loved that strange, stark beauty, the bare grey stone and the grey sky, the few stunted trees. I missed that landscape when I lived away from it, and had taken it for granted when I was there.

I looked across the table at Ted, and I thought of how I had no word to define him, or his relationship to me, and I was glad that it was so. I remembered expressions I had heard used when I was growing up, such as 'going steady'. I found phrases like that completely absurd, they sounded to me as quaint and outmoded as 'keeping company'. I hate convenient empty words, they trap you when you use them. Franca used to call him my *fidanzato*, and I didn't like that either. It was a word that smelt of matrimony, and yet it was vague, too. There was no word to describe the degree of distance and intimacy there was between us. I think I realized then that it was coming to an end, and that we wouldn't be together for much longer, but of course I didn't say anything.

The waiter brought me a little black bitter coffee, the sort I hated when I first went to Italy, but which I grew to love. The pleasure and fascination of other countries has never left me, and I hope it never does. One of my most vivid childhood memories, certainly one of the most pleasant, is of the time a Japanese woman came to visit our neighbours. Until then, I had never met a person from such a distant country, and I was completely fascinated by her. One day I went into the house where she was staying, and she was talking to someone on the phone in her own language, and I was amazed to think that for her all those sounds came so easily, she understood so much and knew so much. She gave me a coloured paper fan that smelt of smoke, and on a sheet of strange paper – pale green, with a pearly sheen to it – she wrote with black ink and a little brush the characters that stood for her name – Yuriko – and mine – Aisling. I said that some day I would go to Japan to visit her, but my brother Jimmy teased me about it. He said that I'd hate it there because I'd have to eat raw fish and seaweed. 'You'll have to eat rice with your dinner, too.' That seemed really odd to me, for I had only ever seen rice cooked in milk and served with prunes. He told me that I wouldn't like the tea, because it was green, and that they wouldn't let me put milk in it, I'd have to drink it black. That made me think it was all a lie, for if the tea was green, how could you drink it black? I told Jimmy I didn't believe him, told him I didn't care, and that some day I'd go away, to see other countries. My image of what those countries would be like was strange and limited, as is often the case with children. For years I thought that New York was America, that is, I thought it was all skyscrapers from coast to coast. I was shocked and disappointed when I found out there were trees and fields too. (I had once told Ted this and he had said, 'Forget about kids, Aisling: I've met

3

adults who think everywhere in America looks like Manhattan.')
When Yuriko went back to Japan, she sent me a postcard,
showing the white cone of Mount Fuji under snow. The sky
behind was deep blue, the foreground full of yellow flowers. I
kept the card, in a safe place, together with the fan and the sheet
of paper with our names on it. For me, they were magical things.
When I grew up I did go away, but I never got to Japan. I had
almost forgotten Yuriko, it was the first time I had thought of her
in years. I wondered where she was now, what she was doing,
and if she remembered me.

Ted interrupted my thoughts. He touched my hands, and,
nodding, said quietly, 'Look over there.'

He indicated three small girls, shabbily dressed and barefoot,
who were each holding large torn pieces of corrugated cardboard. They had approached a smartly dressed woman who was
looking in a shop window, and tugged her sleeve to attract her
attention. At once she was surrounded. All talking at once, the
children held out their hands, demanding alms, while holding
the cardboard out flat to create a little shelf between themselves
and the woman. She was shocked and disoriented to find herself
the centre of attention, when the children suddenly scattered as
quickly as they had gathered, the smallest one triumphantly
waving a slim leather wallet. The woman screamed as she looked
down at her handbag, which hung gaping open from her arm,
having been craftily opened and swiftly rifled by little hands. It
was, of course, all over in seconds: by the time the woman had
started to scream and the people around her noticed what had
happened, the children were out of sight.

Ted shook his head. 'You wonder how they keep getting away
with it. Reminds me of the first time I came to Italy. I had had all
the warnings, and then two days after I arrived, down in the
Forum, exactly the same thing. Three hundred dollars in lire
gone in ten seconds. Losing the money was bad, going to see the
Italian police was almost worse. They just said, "You're the tenth
in today." You could see they'd had it with stupid *Americani*,
getting mugged and then coming to them, as if there was
anything they could do to get the cash back. I almost thought the

4

kids were right, I felt kind of sorry for them, even though the little bastards cleaned me out.'

The city was full of poor children, they were like the pigeons or the wild cats, to be found around all the big monuments, the Colosseum, the Forum, in the big squares and in the streets. Earlier that day, I had seen a tiny girl, without shoes, who walked up and down beside a row of cars which were stopped at traffic lights, begging at the car windows. When the lights changed, she huddled in the middle of the streams of traffic, which made no effort to avoid her, nor, I suppose, did she expect it to. When the lights were red again, she resumed her task, walking patiently from window to window. In the time I watched her, nobody gave her anything.

The preceding evening, just a few hours after we got into Rome, we had been having dinner in a restaurant. We had almost finished the meal, and were talking over coffee and fruit about what we would do the following day. The door opened, and a little girl came in, carrying an armful of red roses, each one sheathed in cellophane. She started to go from table to table, and was rebuffed at each one, the diners often barely looking up from their food to tell her to go away. As she approached our table I said to Ted, 'Buy me one, please.' He asked the little girl how much they cost.

'Two thousand.'

Ted gave her five, and waved away the change. She put the green note in her pocket without a word, handed me a rose, and drifted off to the remaining tables. She had a deep cut above her right eye, her cheek was marked by the last shadow of a bruise, and her whole face showed utter exhaustion. Disappointment and bitterness were stamped upon her features in a way that would have been shocking to see in a woman of forty. She had had enough, and her face expressed the unconscious question: 'If this is life, why was I ever born?' She must have been barely six years old. To show her pity would have been to torment her. The child had reached the door again, and she went out into the night.

I recognized the child. Seeing her made me want to withdraw, and I felt a terrible sense of despair. Some years earlier, I had read an article in a newspaper about child pornography. It was a short article, which described how many children were sold into slavery, how films and photographs were found, showing little children crying, being raped and beaten and cut, showing children being killed. When I read that, it was as if something had fallen over me. Suddenly everything changed, my finger-nails on the edge of the newspaper looked different, the sun on the wall, the feel of my feet in my shoes; everything, everything. I wanted all at once not to be a part of a world where such things could happen. I felt guilty, as though simply by being in such a society, I was acquiescing to its evils. I wanted to do something to show that I was turning away irrevocably from such things, that I could not, would not tolerate them.

All this was brought back to me by the sight of the little girls who stole the woman's wallet. My face must have been as dark as my mind while this chain of thoughts absorbed me, for I realized that Ted was looking at me anxiously. He didn't understand, because he said to me, 'Don't worry, Aisling. You'll be all right when we get there.' For a moment, I didn't know what he was talking about, and then I remembered where we were going the following day. 'It's not that at all,' I told him. 'I am looking forward to going back, although I am a bit nervous too.' He didn't ask me what I had been thinking about, and I was grateful for that.

I'll probably never know what brought Ted and me together, nor what then kept us together for that time. I don't think it matters, I think it's best that it remain a mystery, even to me, or perhaps particularly to me. I don't believe in trying to analyse things like that. I know he was very fond of me, but he was afraid of me too. At first he used to deny it, but then he admitted it. I knew in Rome that it was getting to the point where he was more frightened than fond, and so it probably wouldn't last much longer.

It was too hot to move. I wanted to go on sitting there at the café table. A short distance away, beyond the pavement, the phenomenal traffic of Rome roared past. I was glad I didn't live in

Rome, I didn't think I could ever become used to it. It wasn't the idea of living in a big city that put me off, because I had once lived in Paris. In Rome it was a combination of things – the disorganization, the hellish heat, the constant traffic. I remembered how it had shocked me when I had first arrived there, and, even after having lived in Italy for years, I could still evoke from it that feeling of strangeness. It can feel as if I'm looking at everything backwards, down a long tunnel of time.

I remembered standing one day, waiting to cross the road in Rome. I could smell the dust and pollution and could hardly bear the terrible heat which was coming off the vehicles and beating down like a hammer from the sun; the sun was like bronze. Every so often the traffic would stop, snarled up on itself. Suddenly this happened and I found I was looking into the face of a man driving a big white Landrover. And it was the strangest thing, because I felt that I was looking at a person from an ancient civilization. I saw the whole scene in terms of both time and space, and I saw its absurdity, for there was so much traffic and the jeep in particular was so stupidly big that I knew at once it was all bound to end. It was a completely transient phenomenon, it had only existed for forty years, at most, out of the thousands and millions of years during which there had been life. It was all an aberration, and it was doomed. All the big roads made for it would one day be empty. I looked intently at the man behind the wheel. He looked as innocent as a dead warrior. In his face there was not a trace of doubt, not a hint of the frailty of his own life, his times, his transport. It seemed extraordinary to me that in this city above all, with the evidence all around of broken monuments and vainglorious ruins, people seemed unaware of what would happen. Maybe one of the hardest things is to see beyond your own society, to step out of the collective consciousness of your time, but it teaches you about things as nothing else does. You begin to see your own age not with understanding, perhaps, but with compassion. You see the weakness and smallness of things which are now great or powerful. Sights which might at other times have filled me with contempt now moved me to pity, such as the overdressed women with their jewels and their expensive clothes in the *Caffè Greco*, the pity you might feel for bones found in an ancient tomb, a priceless ring on each fingerbone. I pity them their deaths in a way that they do not pity themselves, and I pity them for their faith in frail mortal things, for not knowing that there will be nothing left but weeds and broken stones.

That afternoon, Ted and I had been to see the frescoes in the Sistine Chapel. They had only been opened to the public again earlier that spring following restoration. Ted had seen them since then, but I hadn't. Looking at them it was easy to believe that they would last for such a long time, but they wouldn't last for ever. No matter how magnificent they are, paintings are made of paint, wood, canvas, clay, and no matter how well they are preserved or restored decay is built into them. Afterwards, because we were so near it, we visited St Peter's. I hadn't been there for years, mainly because I don't like it. As soon as we went in, I could see why. It frightens me. Worse, I feel that I'm supposed to be frightened, that the whole building has been carefully planned to that very end. Usually, I like churches and cathedrals. When I was living in Paris, I used to go to Notre-Dame and the Ste Chapelle quite often, especially in winter. What I was talking about earlier – the facility for stepping out of your own age – is something that these churches lend themselves to well. You can feel a sensibility, a belief in an order which has gone now, but which people long for still, and they visit those churches for exactly that. But sometimes people visit such places because they feel they ought to, because the guidebook tells them to go there. As we walked around St Peter's, I looked at all the other people and I wondered if they liked it, and if so, did they only like it because they felt they should? I suppose all that heavy gilt and marble may appeal to some people. It frightened me. We walked across the wide, empty floors, and looked up at the monstrous, mosaiced cupola. It was too big, and out of proportion. A gothic cathedral, whatever its size, can calm your spirit, and in nature too, a massive tree, a mountain or the ocean itself can have the same effect. I felt, in St Peter's, the terror you sometimes feel in a completely empty landscape.

And perhaps the most foolish thing of all was that I believed I should identify with it. Like the people who felt they ought to admire it, I thought I ought to feel some sort of affinity, because it was 'my' church. I'm still prone to notions like this. I am not a free person. To know it is small consolation.

Nobody was praying. Instead, they were milling about, taking photographs and consulting guidebooks in a variety of languages, and then I noticed a small side chapel, reserved for prayer. I thought of Franca, and I asked Ted to wait for a moment while I went in to pray for her.

On the altar, there was a large gold monstrance, with a host in it, and in front of it, kneeling in an attitude of prayer were two nuns. They were both wearing long blue veils which almost covered them completely, veils which reached the floor with cloth to spare. I couldn't pray: I could hardly contain my anger at seeing those veils, at the crass cynical theatre of it. But then I thought of Franca: she would probably have liked it, been quite impressed by the sight. I think Ted was surprised at how quickly I reappeared.

On that last night in Rome, I couldn't sleep, because of the heat, and because I kept thinking of where we were going the following day, and I was thinking of the churches, all the churches I knew. Some of them still meant a great deal to me, those medieval churches where the raw power of Christianity could speak to me from the anguished face of a painted angel, over the roar of the traffic, in the heat of the night, as I lay there wrapped in a sheet, feeling the pulse of my own heart, and hearing the voice of a tormented angel scream down through the centuries to me.

2

The painting was in the main church of S. Giorgio, 'my' village, as I thought of it then, my village by adoption. Lots of people visit S. Giorgio, although it isn't really famous in itself. It's in central Italy, in Umbria, the part of the country people have in mind when they imagine Italy – pink hill villages, olive groves, vines, frescoes and so forth. People come to visit the general area, and we catch the spillover from some of the more crowded centres. The first time I went to S. Giorgio myself was as a tourist. It was so long ago that I can hardly remember it; I have a memory of the frescoes and of eating an ice-cream with rum in it: a vague, neutral memory. The second time I came back I felt differently about it, and then when I came to live – but more of that later.

It's an extremely old town, and that's one of the things I like about it. It was originally Etruscan, and then the Romans built on it. The main town you see today is medieval. There's a little museum in the square, with the skinny green bronze Etruscan mannikins they dug up there, and a few slabs of Roman stone and old broken pillars, which have never really caught my imagination. S. Giorgio isn't famous for anything, although the people who live there hate you saying that. They think that it's foolish that more tourists don't come, they think that their town is every bit as beautiful as, say, San Gimignano up in Tuscany. I did my bit to promote it: I translated the official guidebook to the town into English. I have to admit it's a hopelessly uninspired document. It brags its onion festival, much to the scorn of other villages around.

No, if S. Giorgio deserves to be known for anything, it's for the fresco cycle in the main church. They're attractive, but by the standards of what you can see in central Italy, they're nothing out of the ordinary. Only the most hardened art historian comes expressly to see them. More often, tour buses stop, with people who've either just been to, or are on their way to, Assisi. The guide will then use the frescoes to explain just why Giotto or Cimabue or Lorenzetti are such magnificent painters, by contrasting them with our poor Maestro di S. Giorgio, and showing them how he fails to fully exploit the space he has, what's wrong with his sense of perspective, why his sense of composition is so unremarkable, his frequent lapses into sentimentality. All this is true, but then, almost everyone looks feeble in comparison to the likes of Giotto, and the Maestro does have his moments. In part, my fondness for the paintings is based on familiarity, and I like some of them very much indeed. There's one in particular of S. Giorgio himself as protector of the village, holding a thing like a covered platter with the lid half lifted, and under it you can see S. Giorgio, completely recognizable with its walls and its church and the bell-tower. I like the crafty old faces of the velvet-hatted burgers kneeling at his feet.

The people who come to S. Giorgio usually do as the guidebook suggests. They visit the church and the museum. They buy bottles of the local wine, take photos, maybe have lunch, and then move on. They think they've seen S. Giorgio, but they don't realize that they've seen only one of its manifestations. Italy is a deceptive country, ours a deceptive village. There are at least three different S. Giorgios.

There's the pretty medieval hill town that people visit in the summer. The same village is completely different in winter, which came as a real surprise to me the first year I was living there. It was late October, and I was walking across the square when I suddenly realized that the crowds of tourists hadn't thinned, but had gone completely. There wasn't a single coach around, nobody taking photographs or writing postcards. The tables were moved in from the streets outside the bars; all the pottery and the other souvenirs were taken in, and most of the little shops were locked up for the winter. The place was deserted, although it wouldn't be true to say that I was the last foreigner there.

Quite a few Germans and English people have bought houses in or near S. Giorgio. Some of them are just holiday homes, but many foreigners have settled there, not all of them happily. Some of those who are quite contented aren't at all well integrated into the community, and they don't even realize it.

S. Giorgio even looks very different in winter. The light is all important here, and on a summer evening in particular, it draws a deep golden creamy colour out of the stones from which the town is built. You don't see that colour at all in winter, when the sky darkens and a bitter wind blows across the square, and makes the narrow streets look gloomy. Many of the visitors who come in summer would be shocked to see the village in winter, because they would see that it's as dreary and provincial as the places they left, and the illusion of summer would be destroyed.

The third aspect of S. Giorgio is there to be seen by anyone who comes at any time of the year, but it's the least considered because people don't want to see it. The part of S. Giorgio I've been talking about so far is the old part of the town, up on the hill. As is the case with almost all the Italian hill villages which are visited by millions of tourists every year, there's a modern part to S. Giorgio. It begins outside the town walls, with a few stray houses, then a few blocks of apartments, then the whole thing spills down the side of the hill and gets properly into its stride, almost as a village in its own right. The railway station for S. Giorgio is down there. When you arrive you can get to the upper village by bus, or if it's not too hot you can walk. People who come to visit generally get the hell out of it as fast as they can, they have a sublime facility for pretending they haven't even seen it.

For the lower part of the town is too like the places they've left, as brash and vulgar and unattractive as modern provincial towns anywhere in Europe. The housing there is generally blocks of apartments made of cement with brown sliding shutters and little balconies. Italy uses more cement every year than any other country in Western Europe, a fact which people generally don't want to know, because it doesn't fit with the image they have, but if you go there and keep your eyes open it won't seem too surprising a statistic. Just beyond the village is a big wide autostrada. It cuts through the plain and goes north past Assisi and Perugia, then on up to Siena and Florence.

The oldness of S. Giorgio means very little to the people who live there. Some of them work in the tourist industry, but most of them work in commerce, in shops or in the big warehouses and factories on either side of the autostrada (as I did, when I lived there, I worked as a translator in a clothing factory). There are factories which make food and clothes, office furniture and tableware. The people who live in the lower town think nothing of the frescoes, and years can pass without their going up to the church. People start work early, and in the evenings after dinner they watch TV. Most families have at least two huge televisions. Sometimes the men go out to the bar, still a male preserve, where the older men play cards in back rooms. The young boys eat ice-creams, listen to Phil Collins on the jukebox, or stand in packs around the door of the bar and have little tussles and fights with each other. Whatever they do, it's done with a sense of restlessness, a lack of repose, wandering in and out of the bar or flicking the remote control of the television from one channel to another. The lower part of S. Giorgio is much more interesting than the upper part, if you really want to know what contemporary Italian life is like; it's a microcosm of so many towns. It lacks that grace which people come to Italy to find, and so they generally chose to ignore it.

The church with the frescoes is in the main square of the old part of S. Giorgio. Directly opposite it there's a small grocery store. The people who owned and ran the shop were a couple called Franca and Davide. They lived in an apartment above the shop, and I lived in an apartment above that again. Franca used to be in the shop all morning, from half past eight until one o'clock, leaning over a big glass counter full of cheese and cold meat. They sold everything you could want. Fresh bread was delivered every day, and the smells of all the things mixed together in a wonderful way – coffee, fruit, *mortadella* and *capocollo*, *parmigiano* and *scamorza*, garlic and floor cleaner – it was extraordinary how well they combined. Franca ran a tight ship. She might occasionally pretend to defer to Davide but in fact she was completely in charge. The apartment in which I lived was for Lucia when she married. As is fairly common practice in that part of Italy, Franca and Davide had made early provision for their daughter. The whole apartment was beautifully fitted out, so they knew that when Lucia got married she would have a home all ready – she would simply move upstairs. Lucia herself was very contented about this, although she regarded it as nothing out of the ordinary. All this was explained to me when first I rented the apartment. Franca told me that she would never rent to Italians, only foreigners, because once locals got in she would never be able to get them out again. When I moved in, Lucia was only ten, and I was amazed when the reason for the apartment was explained to me. I was still there by the time Lucia was fifteen. She helped Franca in the shop in the afternoons and at weekends. Franca herself did very little housework, for they lived with Davide's mother, who was very old but still capable of keeping everything in perfect order. When Franca and Davide closed the shop every day at one o'clock, they came upstairs to find lunch all ready on the table. I got back from the factory about fifteen minutes later, and often, when I was on my way up the stairs, there would be a wonderful smell of *ragu* wafting out from their apartment.

Quite often I would be invited down for a meal in the evenings, or for Sunday lunch. They felt that it wasn't good to eat alone, and it was particularly bad to be on your own on Sundays. If she knew that I was only having something like bread and cold meat for Sunday lunch, Franca would be baffled and vexed. She was a good friend to me. I think we got on well because we were so different, we didn't ever expect to fully understand each other.

I fitted in well in S. Giorgio – eventually, and as well as I would ever fit in anywhere, which isn't saying much. I look very Italian, which did help. I've got long dark curly hair, and brown eyes, and I've also got an unusually dark complexion for an Irish person. I dressed as well as an Italian too. I made a special effort, particularly for my job. I don't think I'd have been respected if I hadn't done that, and although I hated that attitude, I went along with it reluctantly, in a spirit of compromise. You have to, at times, if you choose to live in a country which isn't your own.

Another thing about me is that I'm very small, barely five foot one, and I look very little and sweet, which is a good front. Even now, I'm still constantly amazed at how foolish people can be, how, if you're Irish or little or you've got a soft voice, they'll think they have the measure of you at once, and that you must be really nice. I also speak Italian very well. I studied French and Italian at university in Ireland, but it's from living in S. Giorgio that I became so fluent. I'm even quite good at the local dialect, and I'm a real expert in textile vocabulary. I know all the words and expressions for things like 'bias-cut' and 'piping' and 'set-in sleeve' and 'overlock hem' from my work in the factory. I think I was quite well liked in S. Giorgio. They treated me as a local in all the bars, that is, they didn't charge me the outrageous prices they usually make the visitors pay.

However, the thing that made me a total anomaly in Italy was that I'm a real lone wolf. I've never felt the need for much company. I've never really liked family life, which is one of the great sacred cows of society, and not just in Italy. People act like you're strange, mad or bad if you admit that you simply don't care for it. I built up a life of my own in S. Giorgio, a solitary life. I used to like going down to visit Franca and the others, but I used to enjoy leaving them too, and being upstairs on my own again. A thing I often noticed in Italy was that being together is one of the most important things for people, but it doesn't really amount to much. They might get together for a meal, but then not communicate much – at least, not by my standards of communication. That made it easy for me to socialize, for so little was expected. I used to go downstairs and quietly eat my way from the *antipasti* through to the ice-cream with just the occasional comment about how good the wine was, or to ask where they got the cheese. Every so often somebody would say, *'Va bene, Aisling?'* and I would reply, *'Si, va bene,'* and keep eating.

My job in the factory was a means to an end. I didn't feel hard done by because of that, partly because I know it's more or less like that for everybody. I liked the feeling of being one of the huge mass of humanity that makes and sells things, of being a little part in the process that keeps the material side of life going on, that keeps food on the tables, or in my case, clothes in the shops for people to buy.

I've always placed a high value on my independence, and I've always known what I wanted out of life. I think my aims at that time were fairly modest, and I was pleased with the life I had worked out for myself. My inner and intellectual life was the most important thing, and though I kept quiet about it, almost everything was geared to that. I started early in the factory, at about half past eight in the morning. I hated that, but by one o'clock I was finished for the day. I'd drive back to S. Giorgio and have lunch, and then in summer, when it was really hot, I'd sometimes lie down again in bed for an hour or two. Then after that, or straight after lunch in cooler weather, I would do the extra bits of translating that came my way now and then – things like the guide to the village, or letters and orders for smaller factories that only did a little export work, and couldn't afford a full-time translator. I used to do quite a bit of extra work, and I always tried to get it over as fast as I could, so that the rest of the day was mine.

I used to read an enormous amount when I was living in S. Giorgio. I read in French and Italian as well as in English, and besides fiction and poetry, I read lots of factual books. I'm interested in painting, music, architecture, and archaeology. I liked living in Italy because of the painting and the architecture. I used to go to Rome, to Siena and Florence as often as I could afford it, which was never as often as I would have liked. If you just come to Italy for two weeks you can't get to see things properly. I liked to go to the same galleries and churches again and again.

I used to drive over to Assisi to see S. Chiara and the Basilica of S. Francesco every few months. I was always struck by their beauty, and at every visit I got something new from them. It was the same when I was living in Paris, I used to visit Notre-Dame all the time, and I never tired of it.

So that was the life I had in S. Giorgio. It wasn't easy to get to the point where I had worked out the situation I wanted, and by the time I did, I really appreciated everything I had. Franca thought it was a completely strange and unnatural life for a young woman. She came up to see me late one night not long after I had moved in. I was sitting on my own listening to a record of Bach's St John Passion, and she obviously thought it was a very odd way to spend an evening.

There was a real ambivalence in Franca's attitude to my being in S. Giorgio. She couldn't understand why I left my home, but she could understand why I wanted to live in central Italy, because she couldn't understand why anyone would want to live anywhere else. She was amazed, for example, when I said one time to her that although I was happy in S. Giorgio, I might not always stay there. I thought now and then about moving to northern Italy, maybe to Milan. I'd be able to hear better music, at La Scala and other places.

'Milano? Why go to Milano?' Franca told me that she had been there once, and had hated it. She told me that she had been wearing a white dress, and that when she took it off that night, it was black. Here in S. Giorgio she said, there was everything you could want from life. It wasn't like living right in the country, for Franca herself had grown up in a farm in the hills behind S. Giorgio, and never wanted to go back to such a life, to give up the creature comforts of the town. There was good wine, good food, a nice climate. Of course it was cold in the winter, but they weren't locked in freezing fog for months on end, as they were up in the Pianura Padana, and it was hot in summer, but not scorching, like in Sicily. If I was able to stay in S. Giorgio, she said, and had a good job, why would I ever want to move?

Franca realized that sometimes people had to leave home to look for work. It had been the case with Davide's brothers, two of whom had gone to work in Frankfurt in the early 1960s. They got jobs in an Italian restaurant there. Davide's mother missed them so much, she couldn't get used to them being away, and at

Christmas in particular she would cry inconsolably. Franca didn't think it did either of them any good, even though Mario had stayed and settled there. He married one of the waitresses in the restaurant, a woman from Sicily. ('I suppose we should at least be glad that she isn't German,' his mother said sourly when she heard the news.) They worked very hard and eventually had their own pizzeria in Frankfurt. They also had two children who spoke German and Italian. Franca thought Mario himself had become too like the Germans. The whole family were settled there, and even his mother had long since stopped asking him to come home.

Paolo was another story; he didn't settle there at all. Franca did admire Mario for working hard and getting on when he knew there was nothing for him back in S. Giorgio, but from the day Paolo arrived in Frankfurt, all he wanted to do was go back home again. He did return, too, as soon as he had made some money. But he hadn't made very much, and although he had said he was going to start his own business, all he could afford was a little stall selling *porchetta* opposite the railway station in the lower town of S. Giorgio. The sad thing was, he never really settled after he came back. He had hated Germany, but part of him was still hankering after it. He kept moaning, even to me when I went to his stall for some cold pork on days when I couldn't be bothered to cook, about how much S. Giorgio had changed when he was away, how nothing was the same as it had been. Franca thought he was jealous of Mario, but even more so of Enzo, who hadn't gone away. He had turned out to be the luckiest one of all. He was younger than Mario and Paolo and the family had thought that he might have to go to Germany too when he was old enough. Enzo started selling things to tourists when he was still at school – postcards, maps and guidebooks – and he was ready at the right time, when the tourist market in Italy boomed. He ended up running the two biggest souvenir shops in S. Giorgio; he drove through the narrow streets of the village in a BMW, and he took his holidays in places such as Bali and Kenya.

Even Franca and Davide had been able to improve their lot

because of the tourists. Davide had started off with a tiny, dingy shop, and Franca gave herself – fairly – all the credit for smartening it up, and making it a going concern. She was the one who had bullied Davide into taking down the row of rusty signs outside which said *vini* and *olio di olive* and *olio di semi*. She herself had taken down the faded awning, and replaced it with a bright new one; she had all the shelves inside refitted, to turn the shop into a tiny supermarket. It was Franca who carefully arranged the window in summer, with baskets of cheese and truffles, dried mushrooms and whole hams, to lure in the visitors. In the middle of the window she placed a hand-lettered sign: *Prodotti Tipici*.

Franca viewed the tourists who came to her shop with a mixture of indulgence and contempt. She could well understand why they wanted to come south, and enjoy the good life after slaving away all year in their grey northern cities. Franca had been abroad only once, but as she often said, once had been enough. For their honeymoon, they had gone up to visit Mario in Germany. She had hated Frankfurt. Even though it was summer, the weather had been wet and cold, and she had hated the food – all those deep-fried things, she said, all those horrible sausages! The whole atmosphere of the country unsettled her, there was something too orderly and subdued about it. She remembered they had driven through the mountains on their way north, and saw eerily neat piles of firewood stacked at the sides of the houses. She had said to Davide; 'Wood was never meant to be as tidy as that,' and they had laughed; but she didn't forget it.

After four days of eating sauerkraut off tables they hadn't even bothered to put a cloth on, she had had enough. She told Davide that if he didn't take her straight back to Italy she would get on a train and go by herself. He dutifully drove her to Venice, and they spent their remaining time and money there.

It cured Franca of ever wanting to go abroad again, but she did feel that it gave her a certain understanding of those poor people who came to the village in the summer months. She could well understand how much they liked to sit down in a restaurant in

Italy, and have a waiter put a clean white cloth on the table. Then he would uncork a bottle of good red wine and set a plate of *lasagne al forno* in front of them, and they'd think they'd died and gone to heaven, the poor deprived creatures!

3

When I met Ted, in the late summer of 1989, I had been living in Italy for just over four years. We met in the newsagents of S. Giorgio. I was standing reading the headlines of the *Herald Tribune*, and had my hand raised to lift it from the rack, when someone reached over my shoulder and whipped the paper away. It was the last copy in the shop. I turned round, annoyed. The young American man who had taken it grinned and pointed at the sheaf of papers I was already holding. 'You've probably got enough there already.' I was holding copies of *Corriera Della Sera*, *La Stampa*, *La Reppublica*, and the French paper, *La Libération*. I looked down at them.

'No, I haven't got enough,' I said. 'I want that one too.' I suppose I must have seemed really aggressive, because he looked taken aback, so I smiled, and he thought I had been joking (I hadn't). I decided to let it go, and suggested we have a cup of coffee in the square. I thought he might glance at his paper there, and maybe give me his copy when he had finished.

I should probably explain at this point why I was buying so many newspapers. It was the time when all the changes in the Eastern Bloc were just beginning to break, and I was interested in that, but I'm interested in politics and what's happening in the world all the time. It's an interest that developed after I moved to Italy.

When I first came to S. Giorgio, it took me quite a while to establish myself economically. I had had a good job in France, but when I moved to Italy I took a big risk. I had hoped to do freelance translating, but the pickings were thin. Now people come to me, but at first I had to make a huge effort to find work.

As well as translating, I also taught some English at that time, just to stay afloat. I don't know if my students learnt much, but I learnt a lot. Some of my pupils were children – I taught Lucia, that was part of the deal in my renting the apartment. Franca dreamed of the day when she could put a little sign in her window saying 'English Spoken Here'. I suppose I was lucky, in that it became a little fashion to study English, not just for the people who might have needed it for the tourist trade, but more so for those who didn't need it at all. Of the children I taught, I knew that in most cases their parents had no real interest in learning for its own sake. What mattered was money, money and status. Franca told me once that lots of people only sent their children along to me so they could say to their friends that their son or daughter was taking English lessons with a mother-tongue teacher. Like the piano lessons I had been subjected to as a child, or the dancing and drawing lessons of the last century, it was a middle-class frill, no more than that.

Sometimes when the kids were quietly working on an exercise I'd given them to do, I'd look at their expensive clothes, the brightly coloured backpacks they carried their books in, their transparent watches and their bored faces, and I would think how much of a fluke, how unreal it all was. They had been lucky to be born in Italy at the time of such an economic bonanza. Had they been born some fifty years earlier, they would probably have been living on a farm up in the hills, and their future would have been to work the land, to have faced poverty and possible migration. Instead, these children would probably never be forced to move out of their own region to find work, much less forced to move abroad. While some of the girls might have considered studying the arts at university, all the boys scorned the idea of it. They would study things like engineering, computing, or commercial studies. They went off to Oxford and Hastings in the summer to study English, but for all the money that was lavished on their studies (I charged as much as I dared), the children weren't very motivated, nor were most of the adults I taught.

An exception was Ali, a Moroccan man whom I taught for a

few months. He had been living in Italy for some years, and he spoke Italian well, but now the opportunity had arisen for him to go to the United States. He already had two brothers there, his situation in Italy wasn't particularly good, and so he had decided to move. He came to me for lessons knowing no English at all. He worked so hard – possibly too hard, for he was tense and anxious and felt every mistake to be a terrible thing. There was one lesson in particular that I'll never forget, even though in itself it was like so many others. I was trying to teach him to make offers – 'Would you like a cup of coffee? Would you like a cigarette?' and he was finding it really difficult. We had been struggling along for some time when I noticed the look on his face. He was tired, tense, frustrated, but under that I could see the terrible anger there was in him, anger at the circumstances that had driven him from his own country so that he had to acquire a language that was not his own, and struggle like a child to learn the simplest things. Until then I had felt hard done by in my own fate in Italy, teaching basic English to sullen little brats when I was a qualified translator, but my situation was so much easier than Ali's. I had left Ireland because I wanted to, not because I had to, and had moved from France to Italy because I thought I would be happier there. I wasn't being driven from place to place by sheer economic necessity, as he was.

In a way, it was all very clear. I had more money and better circumstances than Ali, because Ireland is richer than Morocco; and my students were generally better off than I was, because Italy is richer than Ireland. It had no connection with personal merit or hard work, it was a question of politics. Once I had realized that, I could never again see the world in the same way. I became fascinated by how people's lives were at the mercy of political forces: fascinated, but often horrified, too. I took to reading the papers very intently, trying always to recognize what the human cost would be of the things reported there. Then I became aware of how limited and partial the press so often is, so I often bought as wide a range of papers as I could find and afford – Italian, French, English, American – from which I would try to get as broad a perspective on things as possible. The day Ted

23

lifted the paper from before my eyes I had been looking at a photograph of people climbing over the railings into the garden of the West German embassy in Prague. I was so absorbed in this that I was taken aback when the paper was suddenly removed.

So I had a coffee with this American man, and as we talked I remembered something else from my teaching days, a certain type of awareness of the English language. When I was teaching, I was always struck by how polite and cautious a language English is. 'Would you . . . ? Could you . . . ? Shall I . . . ? Do you mind if . . . ? Will I . . . ? Thank you so much. Please excuse me. Don't mention it.' It is a language eminently suitable for not communicating, for talking without making any real connections. At that time I didn't have occasion to speak it very often, although I wrote and read it every day in work. While I was talking to him, I was aware of how much I had taken the Italian language on board, as a sort of protective colouring, like the elegant clothes I affected. I realized how wary I was talking to this American man, and remembering the past, I thought it was wise to be cautious. There can be great scope for deception when you share a language, because it can give the illusion of there being more in common between people than is actually the case. I've learnt to feel uneasy with the instant intimacy you often get with Americans. They tell you all about themselves and their daughter's ectopic pregnancy and the most private details, and an hour later they've forgotten all about you. But I noticed that over coffee Ted didn't pour out his whole life story, nor did he demand mine, and I was very glad for that.

I guessed that he was a few years younger than me, and I found out weeks later that I was correct. He lived in Florence, where he taught art history in a college affiliated to an American university. The students came to study art and architecture, some for a term, some for a year. He had come to S. Giorgio for the day to see the frescoes. As Americans usually are, he was charmed when he heard that I was from Ireland. 'Are you from anywhere near Sligo? My grandfather was from there.' I told him I wasn't, that County Clare was a good bit south of that. He told me he hoped to spend the rest of his life in Italy, he loved it so

24

much. I thought he was very nice. I know that sounds banal, but he was. I could see in him a complete absence of aggression, something I always pick up on immediately. It wasn't a watery sort of yea-saying, but a genuine good nature and kindness. He even gave me his newspaper. I felt bad about that. But I took it.

Afterwards, we went together to see the frescoes. He had already been to the church, but in talking to him I realized he had missed a particular side chapel, so I offered to show it to him. After the warm square, it was very cold in the church. I put a few hundred lire in a little machine, and all the walls were suddenly flooded with light. Looking at the paintings, I was struck, as always, by how immutable they were. There was San Giorgio himself, holding the village on its covered dish, as he had done now for over five hundred years, through so many wars and revolutions. As Ted and I stood there, people in Prague were climbing into the West Germany embassy gardens. They were putting their children and a few suitcases into their tiny cars and driving away from their homes. They didn't know where they would end up, but hoped against hope that it would be better than their present circumstances, thinking that it could hardly be worse, risking their health in a cold, overcrowded garden with poor sanitation. Huge social changes had taken place since the frescoes were painted, including changes in the religious sensibilities of people, so that while the paintings did not alter, the way in which they were viewed was now completely different.

One fresco in particular made me think of this. It showed two life-size figures, the man on the left was writhing, his mouth wide open and he was vomiting a large, black-winged devil. Before him stood a flat, blank-faced friar in a brown habit, his right hand raised. It was he who was casting out the devil from the man, to join the dark, spiky-winged swarm at the top-right-hand corner of the picture. This fresco had shocked me the first time I saw it, and even after having seen it so many times, it could still unsettle me. I used to be amazed at how often I would see people standing in front of it, laughing. I didn't laugh. I took evil seriously. I knew that since I had arrived in Italy I had met no one who was haunted as I was.

A strange thing had happened just after I arrived in S. Giorgio. I had complained to Franca about the pillows on the bed, because they were made of foam-rubber and were too high and uncomfortable. She had looked a bit sheepish, and said, 'I don't know if I can do anything for you, Aisling. I can't get you a feather pillow, because Davide's mother is so superstititious, she won't allow a feather pillow in the house.' I asked what the link was between pillows and superstition.

'Because of the *fattura – il malocchio*, you know, the evil eye.' She could see then that I hadn't an inkling of what she was talking about, so very patiently she explained.

'Here, if someone wishes ill on you he puts a curse on you, and if you have a feather pillow, something strange happens. Some of the feathers in the pillow weave themselves into a knot. A person couldn't do it, and it's a thing that just couldn't happen naturally, it must be supernatural. Davide saw it once, when he was young. His brother Mario was sick when he was about thirteen, really sick, with pains in his stomach. He was wasting away and they thought he was going to die, the doctors had no idea what was wrong with him. And so then they thought it might be the *malocchio*, so they sent for Don Antonio, because he's an exorcist.'

I started at that, but Francesca didn't notice, she just kept on talking.

'So, Don Antonio came and he cut the pillow open, and found this knot of feathers. Davide himself saw it. He said that it was a tight, hard knot, and they were all so frightened when they saw it. His mother began to cry. But Don Antonio knew all the special prayers to say, and from that moment on, Mario began to get better.'

She told me that you could find the same sort of lumps in your mattress, sometimes, and then what you had to do was take it to a crossroads and burn it. She dropped her voice to a whisper.

'They say Don Antonio was called to a house one day, and when he cut open the pillow, what do you think he found?'

'What?'

'A turd,' said Franca. 'Still hot, like it had just been done. Can you imagine how the person in the bed felt?'

I said that I couldn't. I asked her if Don Antonio still worked as an exorcist.

'Yes, but he does a lot less now, because he's so old. He does things in a different way, too. During the last war, Davide's mother saw him exorcise a young girl, right in the church. She saw her screaming and writhing on the floor. I don't think that they're allowed to do it like that any longer. He has a pendulum too. When people are having a lot of bad luck in their lives, their kids are sick and their business going really badly, and they suspect that it might be because someone's put the evil eye on them, they come to see Don Antonio. They come from all over, too, from Tuscany and Lazio, and I even heard that a woman once came down the whole way from Bologna. He holds the pendulum over them, and if it swings in a certain way, then it's bad news. Don Antonio says the prayers to take the curse away.' Suddenly, she looked at me sharply. 'You believe what I'm saying, don't you, Aisling? You don't think I'm making all this up, you aren't laughing at me, are you?'

I replied without a flicker of a smile, 'Oh, I believe you, Franca. I believe in evil all right, you needn't worry on that score.'

There had been times since then when I had thought that I would take myself along to Don Antonio. Would he get the shock of his life, if the pendulum started to loop the loop, or lift itself up, to float in the air, with the ribbon that held it dangling limply? What if I suddenly found myself gripped by one of those terrible spasms, with which I was sometimes afflicted, when I felt that deep anxiety, so that my stomach heaved, and this time, instead of bringing up my dinner, I brought up a real live devil, coming out like a perverted baby, leathery, black and as ugly as sin? I could imagine the reaction of Don Antonio, whom I would sometimes see praying complacently under the frescoes, in the dimness of the church. I thought of how shocked he would be to see the real thing, even after years of swinging pendulums and the odd turd-infested pillow. He would not be able to confront the sight with the same bland confidence of the medieval friar in

27

the painting, to whom such things were all in the course of a day's work. Oh yes, I certainly believed in evil, and I couldn't understand how anyone didn't, all they had to do was to buy a newspaper to read about it in a thousand different forms. I knew there was evil in me.

But I believed in goodness too, and I could also recognize it. Lucia was a good person, she was at peace with herself, and with the world, in a way I could only marvel at.

Once, when I was teaching her, I asked her to describe in English a dream she'd had. She told me she had dreamt about swimming in a beautiful silvery sea, and around her there had been all sorts and sizes of coloured fish, gentle whales, iridescent weed. It was, she said, the happiest dream, it was so lovely to be there, and when she woke up she was still happy. Looking at her face as she told me this, I thought of the threat-filled nightmares that habitually tormented my sleep. I never had dreams like the one Lucia had just described.

The money on the light meter had run out, and the church slipped abruptly into blackness again. Narrowing my eyes, I tried to see the man standing beside me.

'The next time I go to Florence,' I said to this stranger in a loud stage whisper, 'can I come and visit you?'

4

When I travelled away from S. Giorgio any further than about thirty kilometres, I used to take the train. It meant I could relax and look out at the landscape, and think about things. I don't like driving in big cities, and it's almost impossible to find a parking space in Italian towns. So although the train system isn't the greatest, particularly on our line, I don't think it's as bad as many of the Italians used to make it out to be. They just prefer to travel by car, when at all possible. That's another thing that's not widely admitted about Italy. You're told that the most abiding memories you'll bring home are of the Trevi Fountain, or the sun setting over the bay of Naples; but it's more likely to be the memory of being driven at every time you go out, of turning into a street and a car inevitably following you, so you stop and let it past and once that's done, it's quite likely to start reversing back towards you. It's nothing personal, but you can begin to feel that it is when yet another car starts to do a three-point turn on the piece of road where you're standing. The car, the television, chewing gum – they're every bit as important in Italy as they are in America, but these modern obsessions can be hidden behind a screen of past culture, and they get away with it because not many people want to see contemporary Italy as it really is. But if you go to any of the smaller medieval hill towns like S. Giorgio, you see how unsuited they are to traffic. They were designed without that in mind, and it simply doesn't work to try and incorporate it. It's as if you decided to go around in the house on a bicycle. Technically you could probably do it, but you might begin to think that there was something wrong with the house.

When I took the train north that morning in October, it was

still dark, although before long the light came over the land, and I thought of how much I like this landscape in winter, possibly even more than I do in summer. I like it when the soil is turned up in the empty fields: sometimes the earth lies in thick brown clods, sometimes it's as fine as powder. Through the leafless trees you can see the configurations of the land, as if its bones have been laid bare. Just past Assisi, the train rolled slowly over a level crossing, and past the backs of some houses, past hen-runs and small wire pens full of geese and ducks. A mean-faced ginger cat stared at the train as it trundled past, so slowly that I could clearly see the grapes on the vines. Soon, they would be harvested. There were persimmon trees, near enough to touch. I love that tree so much; I love that combination of bareness and fertility, the black, leafless branches and the solid orange fruit, (even though I don't like to eat it, the flesh is too pulpy, and it tastes as though it has already begun to rot). The tree is wonderful, though, with all the fruit like orange lamps; it looks like something a child has decorated.

A few miles further on, I kept a particular lookout for a long row of coloured beehives, in a hollow below a farm. It always gave me a real delight to see them, but they were only ever visible in winter, when there were no leaves on the trees. A little while later, we passed Lake Trasimeno on the left, and everything was blue – the water, the sky, the distant hills, all different muted shades of blue, the sky a colour quite unlike either the heaped clouds of where I lived in Ireland, or the high bare sky of an Italian summer. As we went on north into Tuscany, the land changed, and the rounded hills closed in gently around the track.

I liked the landscape there, and in winter I liked it for that particular combination of bareness and softness. Even though it can be bitterly cold in Italy, I always had the feeling there that winter wasn't going to last long, that it was a brief aberration, while in Ireland you feel that it's the summer that's the freak, having somehow managed to break through the usual wind and rain for a short while.

I have a theory, a strange, maybe a silly theory of my own, to do with landscape: I think that each particular landscape has its own period of time, its own moment in history when it is, or was, most in harmony with the society which exists in it. In Umbria it was the Middle Ages, in Tuscany the Renaissance – the time when the spirit of the land was most complementary to the spirit of the society. I always think of Tuscany as a merchant landscape, able to submit with unparalleled grace to the forces of money and power, in the form they took at that time. You only have to look at the buildings. The merchant towns of pink stone, defensively walled, with solid churches, blend perfectly with the hills, in the way the factories and warehouses of today do not. But the land itself is rich and fertile, yielding easily to cultivation, with its olive trees in neat rows, and its twisted vines. It is so self-evidently a land which has submitted for hundreds of years to the stamp of human power, more than any other I can think of. But it bears that stamp so graciously that people love it for that. Central Italy is one of the most humanized landscapes you can imagine, a place which soothes rather than frightens. It lacks the violence of the sea, and the hard indifference of high, bare mountains.

And much as I liked Umbria and Tuscany, sometimes their prettiness got on my nerves and I missed the violence of nature. I used to think of the Burren, in Ireland, where I grew up. It's a place that can be full of threat, and doesn't feed any illusions about humanity being the most important factor in the natural world. To apply the same theory of landscape and society, the Burren was at that particular point in time thousands of years ago, when the dolmens were built, as stark as the land around them. The people who built them must have understood that land in a way we can now hardly begin to imagine. As the train went north, I thought of the Burren in spring. It was the time of year I most missed being in Ireland, to see the tiny orchids growing in the cracks in the rocks, the flowers so bright against the greyness of the stone. I had shown photographs of the Burren once to Franca and Lucia, but they didn't like it, they thought it was ugly and bleak. The idea of the flowers interested them, but they thought that once a year huge swathes of vivid blooms appeared, and when I told them that no, the flowers were so small, they lost interest again, and I got annoyed. Since then I had avoided talking to people about where I came from: they rarely asked me in any case, and when they did it was always just a conversational reflex, which I could fob off by saying Ireland was very green and, of course, *'bella, tanto bella'*. I couldn't describe the magnificence of the scenery, nor could I explain the psychic violence which I felt there, certainly pre-Christian, perhaps previous to any social life at all.

Was it that that haunted me? I had carried that blackness south with me. It was with me, as irrevocably as the colour of my eyes, and the demons that tormented me seemed to have settled down well in a hot climate. I looked out at the groves of olives, at the red roofs of the houses, and I felt so anxious.

From early that morning, I had had in my mind the image of a woman's body being hanged. It was like a scene in a film, once seen and remembered, and although I found it disturbing to think about it, I could not root it from my mind. The image kept returning to me again and again, unbidden.

I wondered if Ted had found it strange, my calling him up in the middle of the week, to say that I wanted to see him that weekend, and then I realized that I didn't really care. He had sounded pleased on the phone, and I was glad that he was willing to see me. I felt the need of company at that time. During that autumn, I had occasionally felt quite lonely, which was an unusual thing for me. I wanted new companions, a new friend, and there was little chance of that in S. Giorgio. There were Franca and her family, and there were a few other people, all Italians, with whom I got on well, but to whom I wasn't really close. When you make friends with Italian people, there's often an absence of the kind of intimacy and confidences that you expect as a natural part of friendship if you come from Northern Europe. At least that's how it struck me, and for a long time I liked that, I liked the privacy it gave me. It meant that I could be quite close to people without their really getting to know me.

I wasn't popular with the expatriate community in S. Giorgio. When I first arrived, I went along to some of the things they organized, lectures and parties and so forth. Then, one night, I attended the opening of an exhibition of Umbrian landscape paintings by a woman from Cologne. They were watercolours: views of pink churches seen through olive groves, the usual bland, decorative stuff. I remarked how difficult it must be to be a painter in Umbria, because the place itself is such a cliché that it must be almost impossible to produce work inspired by it which isn't also clichéd. The comment wasn't appreciated. As the evening went on, and people made a point of not talking to me, I realized that I'd put my foot in it. Then I realized that I didn't care, and that I was bored. I was always bored at these gatherings, and then I began to wonder why I was there at all. I had nothing in common with those people, and after that evening, I stopped pretending that I did. They began to think of me as cold and aloof, which was fair enough. I wasn't friendly to them, but I didn't want their friendship, and if they had known me, really known me, I don't think that they would have wanted mine. I've lived away in two countries now, albeit in Europe both times, and if I've learnt anything, it's that you can't be too careful of foreigners living abroad. You often find they're strange people, that they're not happy in themselves, that they're trying to run away from something, and that they're only half aware of all this. There can be a great sense of unreality about them, something I always try to avoid. They always get together to whinge and moan about the country they've chosen to live in, the damn French and the bloody Italians, as if they were doing the nation in question a great favour by being there. Although it may not sound like it, I'm not setting myself loftily above these people: some of the things I've said about them, like their trying to escape from certain things, are true for me too, but it doesn't interest me to be around people like that.

Most of the time I was happy on my own, but that autumn I was lonely, and I did want company. I liked Ted, and I thought it was ideal that he was living in Florence. If I went there and the whole weekend was a disaster, I could go back to S. Giorgio and no one would ever know anything about it, and Ted and I need never see each other again.

The train was on time. I felt nervous as we pulled into S. Maria

Novella Station, because in spite of my rationalization, I dreaded a disastrous weekend. I try to be cut and dried about such things, but it isn't really possible. The station was busy, as it always is. Even out of season, when there are no visitors in places like S. Giorgio, cities like Venice and Florence still have tourists. There were a few blonde backpackers wandering about on the platform, holding plastic bottles of mineral water in their arms; there were some nuns in long cream habits; there were super-elegant people with smart, co-ordinated luggage. Above all this there was the usual torrent of train announcements, the mellifluous list of city names – *Bologna, Milano, Brindisi, Roma, Terontola* – and the occasional announcement in English. Just as I was stepping down from the train, I saw Ted, at the very moment he saw me. A man with one of those big deep trolleys from which they sell drinks and sandwiches almost ran him down. The man with the trolley paid no heed, but pushed on up the platform, bawling at the top of his voice, '*Panini, gelati, patatine, bibite, acqua minerale . . .*'

There was something wrong with me that day – more wrong than there usually is, if I can put it that way, for the world often seems out of kilter to me. I had been to Florence many times before, but that Saturday it seemed different, it was hyper-real, the way things in a dream can appear more real than things in life. I told myself I should have had something to eat before leaving S. Giorgio, and then I saw how foolish a thought that was. As if the light-headedness and the gnawing feeling of terror that there was in my stomach, and the weird look of everything, could have been eliminated simply by having had a cup of coffee and a cake three hours earlier.

My initial reaction when I saw Ted was sheer terror. I wished that I had seen him before he saw me, so that I could have sneaked off and hidden. I could have rung him later in the day and pretended still to be in S. Giorgio, could have told him I missed my train that morning, and then skulked around the city hoping not to meet him. Even when he walked up to me, I wondered for one wild second if I could just smile at him and say,

'Why, hello!' and then walk straight past him, as if seeing him there was pure coincidence. After all, he was almost a total stranger to me.

But he saw me as soon as I saw him, and he headed straight for me, so there was no chance to do any of these crazy things. He came up and said 'Hello' and took my bag, and then I saw that there was nothing else for it, so I settled down to the day that I had set up for myself, and which now frightened me so much.

We went straight to a café for breakfast, and although I felt much better for some coffee and a cake, it didn't stop me from feeling nervous and strange. We talked about the usual nothings you talk about when you meet someone off a train, but we talked about them for longer than usual – the weather, how long the journey had taken, whether or not I was tired, had I had a good journey, and other classic topics of non-conversation. Ted appeared very happy that I had come to Florence for the day. He asked if there was anything in particular I wanted to see or do while I was there. I said I would like to walk up to Piazza Michelangelo, to look out over the city, as it was a bright day.

Florence is a strange city – although everywhere and every-body are strange, I suppose, according to your particular perception, and even the oddest things can appear normal, if that's how you choose to see them. What I find strange in Florence is the effect of tourism there. It is one of the most beautiful cities in Europe, and you can buy there some of the ugliest things possible, like a plastic ashtray with a reproduction of a Botticelli on it, so that you can stub your cigarette out on Venus's breasts. A thing like that is so crass that you can hardly believe that it's not deliberate. It becomes a work of art in itself, deconstructing the accepted canon. As we crossed over the Ponte Vecchio I said to Ted how I always was struck by this aspect of Florence every time I visited it. You see so many visitors there, particularly around the Ponte Vecchio area, and they've come from all over the world, often during the only period of free time they have all year and at great expense. And yet when you look at them you have no feeling at all of their being happy, or even reasonably contented. You just see this tide of passionless life, with crowds of people looking through each other, bored and listless, gazing at the identical shop windows along the bridge, with their silks and gloves and gold jewellery. Ted said that he often felt the same looking at people who dripped money: you could sense the boredom and sterility there was in their lives.

'But if you really want to see miserable people,' he said, 'you should go to Venice. It's like Christmas – you know what I mean? There are times and places which are supposed to be happy, happy, happy, and if you feel bad there, you feel guilty too, for not feeling the way you think you ought to. Venice is full of people who're as miserable as hell, because their expectations for the place are so high that there's no way reality can match it.'

He was right. When we got up to the Piazza, we stood for some time leaning on the parapet, looking out over the roofs of the city. Here I was with someone I liked and who gave every appearance of liking me, and we were in Florence together, and yet I still felt troubled and anxious. I'm not a person who has much talent for happiness, but I remember one of the best moments in my life. It was in Paris, where I used to live. It was a wet weekday morning in March, and I was standing up at a bar counter having a quick coffee on my way to work. I remember I was tired because I hadn't slept well the night before, and then I caught sight of myself in the mirror behind the bar. I saw myself as if I were a stranger, as if I were someone other than myself, and in that moment I realized that I had everything I wanted in life. I had been in Paris for about four months then. I had my job, a little apartment, I had money in my purse to pay for my coffee, I was an adult. I felt free. And with all these things I felt a sublime happiness, which was all the more intense for the banality of the surroundings – the tattered pricelist on the wall, the rain on the window. I don't really understand why I felt like that at that particular moment, but I didn't try too hard to understand, it was a mysterious feeling, and I thought that it was best not to try to analyse it. I was just grateful. I've often remembered that morning when times have been bad, for if you know that such moments of peace have been possible, you know that they might happen again. And if you're really troubled in your soul, it can mean so much to know that.

Later, when we were walking back into town, we passed a group of street traders, Nigerians and North Africans, who sat silently by their wares, which were set out before them – sunglasses and hairslides, fake designer bags and sweatshirts, and cassette tapes. Ted said, 'I feel sorry for them: they're not welcome here.'

'I know,' I replied. When I was teaching English in the past, one of my students said that he had been to England the previous summer. He had very little money, and had difficulty in finding a room, so he ended up in a hostel. It was full, but they let him bunk down in a sleeping bag on the floor of one of the rooms. There were six beds, he told me with a shocked air, and all the people in them were African. I said, 'Maybe when they got back to Africa they told their family and friends, "When we were in London, we stayed in this joint that was so cheap and tacky that there was an *Italian* sleeping on the floor of the bedroom."' But my irony was lost on him.

I had a feeling that I would have to give account of myself to Ted, later on that day, and over lunch I decided that I would tell him about what happened when I was in France. Over a couple of plates of *spaghetti alla carbonara*, Ted kept asking me about Ireland. He couldn't understand why I'd left. 'Everybody says it's such a beautiful country.'

'It is,' I said, 'but sometimes that isn't enough.' I had had my own reasons for wanting to go away. I found life at home too homogeneous. Almost everybody I knew had been to the local convent school, their experience of life was within a certain limited ambit, and I didn't like that. My leaving had been premeditated, and deliberate. I had studied languages so that I would be able to move to another country with more facility. But on another level, my leaving was purely instinctive, as automatic as the new-born animal's search for food, as mysterious as the migratory impulse of birds. It was all painfully clear and simple. I had had so many unhappy experiences in Ireland, that I wanted to put distance between myself and that place. There was a day a few months after I'd moved to France when I was lying in bed late one night, half asleep, when I suddenly realized what I had done, what I had succeeded in doing. Here I was in a little apartment in Paris, a place so unlike where I'd grown up, and the room was full of my clothes, my books, my things. It was extraordinary that they belonged to me, because this was what I had wanted so much, and it was hard to believe that I had actually got it.

It didn't last. The human capacity for irrationality, for breaking up things which you've worked so hard to build, is remarkable.

'So how long were you in Paris?' Ted asked. I told him that I had been there for three years. After college in Ireland, I had done a course in Paris to become a translator. I had been given a placement in a small factory, which went well, and became a full-time job. I rented an apartment in an unremarkable part of the city, and I worked very hard. The weeks were quiet and dull, but I made a point of enjoying the weekends. I used to go to exhibitions and galleries, and sometimes I would get right out of Paris, to the woods or to the coast. I went to Chartres and to Rheims several times, and I visited all the cathedrals in the city as often as I could. My life was much as it was to be later, when I was living in Italy. I did have a few friends, but it was very much a solitary, internal life, the life of someone without great ambition, someone who wanted peace and privacy, above all the life of someone who just wanted to be left alone.

And then, after I had been there for two years, I did the most stupid thing. I fell in love.

Well, it wouldn't have been so stupid if I really had loved him, but as it turned out, I didn't.

'This man was an American too,' I said to Ted. By this stage we were eating fruit, and had ordered coffee. I was carefully cutting up a pear. When I was much younger, I was wary of men, as wary as a dog that's been beaten. I couldn't understand women who wanted to get married, couldn't understand women who thought that a man could make them happy. Then I met Bill. He was interested in all the things that I liked too: painting, music, architecture. We went to concerts and visited galleries together; we used to sit in the Luxembourg Gardens and talk, or walk through the streets late at night in the rain, looking at all the people and speculating on their lives, laughing at silly things. It gives me no pleasure to remember all this now. I have no happy memories from that time, instead it makes me feel ashamed to think of how stupidly I was taken in. He was doing a language course when I met him, and was in France indefinitely. Before long, he moved into my apartment. Bill was from Missouri, and he told me all about his family, about how his parents had divorced when he was ten, about his mother's drink problem, about other girlfriends he'd had in the past. I trusted him completely, and told him all about my life too, things I had never been able to talk to anyone about until then. When it was all over, I realized that he was like a lot of Americans, that he'd have told his most intimate life history to someone on a bus, to the newspapers, to any stranger. His confidences didn't mean a thing. But mine did.

Then one day he came home and told me that a guy he knew was going down to Aix-en-Provence, and had asked him if he wanted to come along. This friend knew a painter living just outside Aix, there was room in his house for Bill too. He was delighted. He'd always wanted to see Provence. I had spent a holiday there, and had told him all about it. He told me now that he'd had enough of Paris. City life was beginning to get on his nerves, he was glad to be going to the country. I didn't say anything. I couldn't believe it. I had thought he loved me. I had thought that because he had moved in with me and we had been so close that he was in some way committed to me, and when that word 'committed' came into my mind, suddenly I understood, and saw what a fool I'd been.

Later, what I regretted most was how predictable and clichéd everything was that happened next. The scene I created, all my stupid tears, 'But you said . . . but I thought . . .' all that nonsense that's been said a million times in the past, and that'll be said a million times again. I couldn't believe that I was being so wounded by something that was so banal. I hated myself for crying, for having been so stupid as to have let all this happen, for not having seen it coming.

Bill was amazed. He said that he had had no idea that I would react like this. He thought that we could still be friends, which meant that he thought he could rely on me for free meals and accommodation next time he was passing through Paris. I told him to get out of my apartment immediately, but I didn't tell Ted how I had persuaded him to go: by picking up a kitchen knife and saying, 'Because if you don't go now, I'll kill you.' I said it like I meant it, and he left.

When he came back for his things the next day, I punched him in the face as hard as I could. It wasn't that I lost my temper, it was completely premeditated. I had spent all night thinking of how much I wanted to hurt him, really hurt him, to get my own back. I'd been afraid I'd fudge it, but I didn't. I cut his lip against his teeth, and got great satisfaction from the look on his face when he saw the blood. Ted listened to all this quietly. 'How do you feel about him now?' he asked me. I said that I still hated him. If I heard that something terrible had happened to him, that he was seriously ill or even dead, well, I wouldn't actually be glad, but I wouldn't be at all sorry either. 'So it's stupid to think I ever loved him, isn't it?' I said.

After Bill had gone, I realized that he'd ruined my life there. I had always liked my apartment, but now I associated everything in it with him. He'd contaminated it for me by his presence. It was the same with all the places I liked to visit in Paris and the things I enjoyed doing. They no longer held any pleasure for me, because they reminded me of him. I thought of the life I had so carefully built up for myself and how I had let it all be destroyed. I hated him, but he was gone. I hated myself, but I couldn't escape from myself. I had thought that he was helping me to overcome all that, and now it was worse than ever it had been. I blamed myself for having been so gullible, and trusting. Even now I can hardly bear to think of how bitter and lonely I felt at that time.

A few months later, in the summer, I had holidays to take from work. My mother wanted me to go back to visit her in Ireland. I didn't want to go, I was afraid to go back. I was afraid that if I went there, I would really see what a failure it had all been, my attempt to make a life for myself, to mend things. I could hardly bear it in Paris, but to think of these things back in County Clare would be overwhelming. Maybe I would be trapped into staying there. So even though my mother pleaded with me, by letter and by phone, I said no, and set off for two weeks in Italy.

It restored me, to some extent. I went to Florence, then down to Umbria, to Assisi, to S. Giorgio. Only when I was away from the city did I realize how exhausting the daily round was, how crushed I had become by the endless journeys on the Metro, by the crowds, the work, the whole life I led there. I had no interest or energy left to do anything at the weekends. I had stopped going to the galleries after Bill left. But in Italy I was looking at paintings again, and they meant a lot to me, I realized that I needed that in my life. I visited the frescoes in S. Giorgio, and then sat down at a café in the main square and had an ice-cream. While I ate it, I felt lulled by the sunshine, the palpable softness of the life going on around me. I realized that I dreaded going back to France, that my life there was dead, and held nothing more for me. Then, in a window above the grocery shop on the other side of the square, I saw a bright pink card, on which was written, 'Apartment to rent.'

Within a month I was living there. Within two months, I realized that I had made a big mistake.

Perhaps in the long term things worked out as well as could be expected, but at first it was so difficult. I had acted completely on impulse. I gave up a good job in Paris, through which I had accumulated reasonable savings. These were rapidly eaten into when I moved to Italy, much more than I had expected. I've always known how vital it is for a woman to have enough money, and it worried me to see it melt away like this. I had foolishly hoped to find another translating job, but it turned out to be much more difficult than I had expected. For months I had to scrape by on whatever I could find, translating, teaching English at all hours of the day just to make ends meet. It was such a struggle and I was so worried about money that at least it took my mind off worrying about other things, like mere loneliness. I had no car at first, because I couldn't afford one, and I felt trapped in S. Giorgio. I had visited it only in summer, and I couldn't believe how quiet it was off season. I stood out much more than I cared to, and the locals couldn't understand what a young woman was doing living there on her own. Franca and her family took a liking to me, they helped and befriended me from the first, and that made a big difference, but I didn't make friends with any of the other foreigners living in S. Giorgio.

Then my mother died. I felt guilty, because she had wanted me to go home to see her and I hadn't gone, and now I'd never see her again. I went home for the funeral, and I felt that everyone there, including my brother Jimmy, felt I had been selfish and heartless to stay away. Jimmy was older than me, we had never had a lot in common. He lived up in Dublin, and now that our mother was dead the family home down in Clare was empty. He pretended to be all surprised when I said that I wouldn't move home now, as if that was all I had been waiting for, for my mother to die so that I could have the house. I could feel the disapprobation of everybody because I hadn't been the warm, loving daughter, or rather, because I hadn't behaved as they thought a loving daughter should. I didn't get on with my father at all, but I had been fond of my mother. I regretted any pain I caused her, but I don't see how things could have been different. When I got back to Italy and looked at my life there I thought: Was it worth it? I had made such a huge effort of will to make a life of my own, and what had I ended up with? A rented flat, a few sullen students, being snickered at in bars in the village.

Things got better: I suppose they had to, I felt that they couldn't have got much worse. I decided that I would do best to stay put for at least another six months, to try to make a year of it in S. Giorgio. I had enough sense to realize that I had made a hasty false move from Paris, and I knew that I couldn't afford to make another. There was no place to which I felt particularly drawn. I had no reason to be in S. Giorgio, but I had no better reason to be anywhere else. I couldn't go back to France, and for now there seemed to be no other openings in Italy. I decided to keep going throughout the winter, and then in spring I could reconsider the situation.

But by spring, things had changed. By an odd set of circumstances, my life began to improve. A woman called Fabiola started to have English lessons with me. She took a liking to me – God knows why, for I barely registered on her consciousness. She thought I was *carina*, *simpatica*, which shows how little she knew me. Fabiola had one of those smiles which makes no connection with the person being smiled at, its sole function to state 'Aren't I lovely!' From the first she irritated me, with her gold pencil, her leather briefcase, bought specially for her English books, the way she dressed up for lessons with me as if she were going to a wedding. That struck me as particularly foolish, as the lessons themselves were such a complete non-event. She was by far my slowest student. Although she had studied English at school for five years, we had to begin again at zero, and in all the time I taught her, she never made much progress. Her husband owned a clothing factory down on the plain below S. Giorgio, and Fabiola had no financial worries, her only problem in life was to fill her empty days.

One day, at the end of the lesson, we were talking about a suitable time to see each other again, and Fabiola remarked, 'If my husband knew how well you spoke Italian he might give you a job in his factory. He needs someone to translate letters and things for him.' I immediately pursued this throwaway comment, but Fabiola tried to dismiss it. She said airily that he was looking for a translator, 'But if you get the job, maybe you won't want to give me English lessons any more, and where would I find another teacher as sweet as you?' She smiled radiantly, picked up her briefcase, and was about to leave. I couldn't believe it. I blocked her way. 'Of course I'd go on giving you lessons,' I said. 'Even if I stopped teaching everybody else, I'd still teach you, if I was working in your husband's factory. You will mention it to him, won't you?' I did my best to give her a big smile – in truth, I could hardly keep my hands off her. She was quite liable to let this chance pass me by, for some stupid whim about lessons, which she could lose interest in at any time. 'If I tell Pietro he has to give you the job, then he has to give you the job,' she said. I knew she was perfectly capable of forgetting all about it as soon as she left my apartment, but Pietro got in touch with me two days later, and in a short while, to my enormous relief, I was back in regular employment.

Things got better then. I had a steady income, regular hours, and I could take on as much or as little extra work as I wanted. I was more used to S. Giorgio by that stage, and S. Giorgio was more used to me. I decided to stay for a couple of years, to establish myself again financially and to get some work experience, and to build up a life for myself, as I had done in Paris. Almost five years later, I was still there. It wasn't that I loved Umbria so much, rather I got caught up in the gentle, soporific round of the years, which can be as hard to break out of as a dream. By late 1989 I was certainly thinking about moving on, but had made no definite plans to do so. I felt I ought to go, if the rest of my life wasn't to drift by in a haze.

'So that's it,' I said to Ted. It was a strange experience talking to him in this way, even though I didn't tell him everything, and there were some things I couldn't express, like the anger of those last months in Paris. I couldn't explain to him the rage that there was in me, that was always there, no matter where I was, a force stronger than myself, and which I didn't fully understand. It was interesting for me to look back over my past like that. I didn't often do it, and it was strange to consider it, after all those years, to see what had changed and what hadn't. It interested me so much on my own account that I hardly took any notice of what effect the things I was saying had on Ted. But he could never say that I had pretended to be something other than I was – *he* couldn't say that I had taken him in.

The table in front of me was covered with the leftovers of a meal – broken bread, an empty carafe, fruit peelings, two crumpled linen napkins, two thick white cups, ringed inside with coffee. Ted said, 'I know it must have been painful for you, but I'm sure that guy in Paris didn't mean to hurt you as much as you think he did.'

'I know,' I said. 'I'm out of step with everybody. That's what people I knew in Paris told me at the time. The way people relate to each other has changed. But it's not just as if you can change like that – I couldn't, anyway.'

The hanged woman was still lurking in the corner of my mind. They say that you're responsible not just for everything you do, but for everything you see. I felt as if I had seen this woman, had broken some taboo by looking at her, and this was to be my punishment. The dead woman would haunt my mind. I made a huge effort to look across the table and focus on Ted. I wondered how much he had understood of what I had said – that is, I wondered to what extent he saw it as I saw it. It probably looked very different to him. He had most likely had relationships like the one I had described, the difference being that they had been with women who had not thought as I had, women who were capable of being close to someone without putting too much emotional commitment into it, knowing from the first that it was a transitory thing, and that it would be foolish to feel aggrieved when it ended. And I could see too that Ted wasn't a wicked person. Far from it: he was a much better person than I would ever be, and perhaps the man I'd known in Paris wasn't wicked either. But he had been the cause of such pain to me, and I felt that he should have known it. I could never forgive him, I didn't even want to try.

When we came out of the restaurant, it was still very quiet in the streets. That lunch-time hush that descends upon Italian cities was still in effect, the shops closed, the streets deserted, so we went to Ted's apartment. He lived near the centre of Florence, in a few attic rooms in a high yellow building. It was a simple, untidy place, with papers and books scattered around. I was glad to see that. I did try to hide the thoroughness with which I was taking everything in – the cream jug on the window sill, the crumpled envelopes with letters sticking out of them, the ailing potted plant on the shelf. I don't like tidy homes, and I just can't stand places that have been subject to interior design. The sort of things you see in homes and gardens magazines and that people really drool over, I absolutely hate. I don't, for example, like Fabiola's house, although I'm sure she thinks that I do, because it's a beautiful place by conventional standards, therefore everyone should like it. That's just what I have against it. She's got a marble-topped table and a lamp that just looks like a plain steel pole and some angular black chairs. There are marble floors, and everything else is black, white and silver, made of leather, chrome or ebony. Everybody oohs and aahs about it, but I think it's sterile and uncomfortable. Fabiola herself only likes it because it's what she thinks she's supposed to like. She hasn't a thought in her head that hasn't been put there by social and commercial forces. I liked the small-scale scruffiness of Ted's apartment. I told him so, and he laughed. He said that although it wasn't very big, he had been lucky to find something he could afford so close to the centre. I asked him how he had found it.

'Through a friend of a friend: how you get everything in Italy,' he said. Looking at his possessions, I remembered how, when I was a child, things which belonged to other people often fascinated me – a hairslide or some furry slippers, foolish things like that. I would long to possess such things myself, but on the few occasions when I managed to obtain an identical object, it no longer had the magic which had drawn me to it in the first place. Its mystery and attraction were immediately lost, simply by my possessing it.

'What sort of place do you have in S. Giorgio?' I described my apartment to him. I told him I liked it, but that sometimes it was too noisy.

'That's a problem when you live in a noisy country,' he said. 'Yes,' I replied. 'I suppose it could be worse.' Sometimes it didn't bother me when Franca and Lucia would be shouting and roaring in the stairwell, and the television was on full blast from early morning until late at night. Sometimes it got on my nerves. What really annoyed me though was when Franca set herself up as a model of happiness, and said that I too could be as happy as she was. She was always telling me that I thought too much. It only complicated things, and made you miserable. I hated it when she talked to me like this. It was certainly true that I wasn't happy a lot of the time, but I didn't believe that putting your brain on ice could make much significant difference. If the price of consciousness is misery, then I'll take that any day, rather than dumb bliss. I can't stand it when people try to make you be the same as they are, as if their own lives are so wonderful.

Sometimes I used to think that Franca was like a great big tabby cat, living on pure instinct. I once had a cat when I was growing up in Ireland. It was going to have kittens, and I realized one day as I watched her sitting licking her paws that she wasn't at all concerned about it, she wasn't getting ready for it or worrying about the future. She wasn't even aware that she was going to have kittens. And then when they were born, she was perfectly contented, and stayed in her box with them and looked after them. She sat over them purring, and growled a little when I put my hand in to try and touch them. Six months later, she was killed. The kittens didn't miss her. Often when I looked at Franca, I would remember that cat.

There was a glass egg on the table, and I picked it up. I asked Ted if it was Murano glass, and he said that it was. Franca had a Murano glass decanter and six matching liqueur glasses that she got on her honeymoon in Venice. They were made of dark red glass, and were all hand painted with flowers – really florid. I know that she never used them, not even once, in all the years she was married. She kept them locked up in a glass-fronted cabinet. I know such a thing is outmoded and foolish, like the idea of a best parlour, but it appeals to me. We had a china cabinet at home in Ireland. I like the idea of having all those bits of glass and delft and keeping them locked up for years and years. They became a sort of witness to all the *sturm und drang* of family life; they give you a fixed visual point, even if it is only in the form of a carnival glass tea-set, or a silver-plated sweet dish. We were never allowed to use them, and as a child, it was as if they didn't even belong to us, they had that mystery of other people's possessions. As I grew older, I liked them even more, for their worthlessness, because the only value they could have was sentimental. Sometimes when I was in Fabiola's house, and I looked at her cold and costly fixtures and fittings, I'd think of those things we had at home, like two delft pigs hugging each other, one for salt and one for pepper.

47

'I don't like things that just have monetary value,' I said to Ted. He was standing over by the window watching me. I was still holding the glass egg. 'My grandmother used to say about people, "Money's their God," and in Italy I feel like I know people for whom that really is true, and they make no attempt to hide it. I often think about that when I'm in the streets, when I visit a city like Rome or Florence. In a shop window you'll see maybe a pair of shoes on a little platform, all cleverly lit like they were a holy relic, and you'll see people looking in the window, and it's like they're almost awed. I want to say to them – it's only a pair of shoes, for crying out loud, only a belt or a handbag or whatever it happens to be. In a few years' time all these things will be worn out or they'll just look foolish. Sometimes when I see people in the street I feel pity for them, as if I'm looking at them from a thousand years away. Do you know what I mean?'

He said that he understood. I wasn't sure that he did, but I decided that, for now at least, I would believe him.

5

I won't say anything about whether or not I slept with Ted that night. Even if I did say, it would be foolish to believe me, because everybody tells lies about sex, and I'm no exception. What I will say is that it took me a long time to fall asleep, which is usual when I'm away from home. I lay awake far into the night, looking at the window. There was a big moon. It made a pale square of light on the floor, and I remembered a dream I once had. In it, there was a huge flat golden moon, which was low in the sky behind a leafless tree. I was able to reach out and touch the moon; I put my arm through the branches and pulled it out of the sky. It came down as smoothly and as easily as a circle of silk. Shimmering, golden, it hung limp in my hand, but now there was no light. I remembered I had felt happy when I woke up, because the dream had been a good one. When I looked at the moon over Florence I hoped I might dream it again, but I didn't dream at all that night. I didn't mind, because I could so easily have had one of my usual nightmares, and I was grateful that I didn't.

The following morning, even though it was October, it was dry and bright enough for us to have breakfast sitting outside. We went to Piazza Santo Spirito, which was all but deserted, and quiet but for the noise of a television from behind a high, shuttered window, its frenetic gabble of trailers and ads muffled by distance. We didn't talk much. I'm always quiet and sleepy in the morning, it takes me a long time to shake off the night. I had coffee and a big custardy cake, which I pulled apart with my fingers and ate slowly. If I could, I would eat things like that every day, but I only treat myself occasionally. I let my eyes wander over the high pale buildings around us, the spotted trunks of the plane trees, and the flurrying crowds of pigeons which gathered around a fountain.

On the way to the café we had passed the place where Dostoyevsky had finished writing *The Idiot*. I looked at the building out of the corner of my eye, and thought of the day I first saw it, years before, on a visit to Florence. It's an unassuming yellow house opposite the Pitti Palace. The only unusual thing about it is the stone plaque that tells whoever cares to know that Dostoyevsky finished writing the novel there in 1868. I had been tempted for a moment to point it out to Ted, but I didn't. It's so precious to me that I wouldn't have known how to react if he had just said 'So what?' or 'Big deal.' Often I had watched crowds of people drift past the house and never look up, paying no more heed to it than to any other building around, but to me it was precious. If Ted didn't share that appreciation (and I felt quite sure that he wouldn't), I thought it would be a desecration to draw his attention to it. So I said nothing, we walked on.

On one side of the square where we were sitting, there was a church. On the façade was a memorial to the fallen of two world wars, with a list of the names of the men of the parish who had been killed. The whole thing was surmounted by a dusty wreath, decorated with golden baubles like Christmas-tree ornaments, and their brightness only made the leaves and the ribbon look even more faded and dull. There was a war memorial in S. Giorgio too, with a flagpole. The cord which runs down the side of the pole pings in the breeze, it makes the same sound that the masts of boats make when they're all pulled in to harbour on a quiet night. When I passed the war memorial in S. Giorgio, I always used to think of the sea.

The church itself looked old and neglected. Weeds and tufts of tough grass grew in cracks on the steps in front of it. Mass must have ended, because a congregation was leaving the building, twenty people at most, the majority of them elderly women. Then I saw two other people crossing the square, one of them also an elderly woman dressed in black, walking slowly with the aid of a cane. She was arm-in-arm with a middle-aged woman, whom she was hectoring relentlessly. Oddly, because of her beaten, defeated look, the younger woman looked the older – that is, as if her soul had aged. She was dressed in a suit, dressed with neatness and precision, but was not at all elegant. Her clothes were drab and unflattering, her short hair set in a rigid style, her face submissive, tired. As they walked past us, I could hear their voices, the old woman releasing a torrent of angry language, the other woman patiently interjecting every so often, *'Si, Mamma. Si, Mamma.'* In my mind's eye, I could see the apartment they had just left. I had been in Italy long enough to imagine it down to the last detail – the clean, cold rooms, the glass-topped table with a lace runner and an ugly piece of ceramic on it, which, twice a day, the daughter would laboriously clear away, and then set the table. I could see the white stone floors which, after meals, would be ruthlessly swept, then polished. On the sideboard there would be a framed black and white photograph of the elderly woman and her husband, taken years before, but she would still not look young in it, would look hard and stern. Beside the photo would be a green plant, and there would be other green plants around the house, some of them huge. Their beds would be neat, narrow, perfectly made, and there would be a big multi-channelled television, which they would watch impassively for hours every evening. And so their lives would pass.

The two women had reached the top step of the church. They pushed the worm-eaten inner door, and the huge blank façade swallowed them up.

'Ted,' I said, 'did you know either of your grandmothers? Do you remember them?'

'Grammy? Do I remember Grammy? Who could forget her? Grammy was like a Marine with lipstick. Or rather, she would have been if she'd worn lipstick.' He laughed and was quiet for a moment. 'Funny you should ask about her. I think about her all the time. Well, a lot of the time, anyway. I guess I think about her to know what I really do think about her.'

He told me that 'Grammy' was his mother's mother. He never met his father's mother, she died in 1942, before his parents had married, but from family legend she was every bit as tough as the grandmother he knew. The lies of the past! I never cease to be amazed by the discrepancy between the myth of womanhood and the reality of it. What family doesn't have a sepia print of some doe-eyed creature, all roses and poses, in her high-necked white blouse and long dark skirt, pretending to read a book while her sister leans sweetly over her, or playing the piano while her sister turns the pages.

Looking at these submissive shrinking violets, who would ever guess the tales that are handed down in families, of how they drove through the lives of their children like tanks, making wounds which it would take generations to heal. Ted said that he thought a hundred years wasn't a long time at all – in human terms, in terms of the individual, yes, it's usually longer than life itself, but in terms of a family, it's very short.

'I look back at my grandparents,' he said, 'and I feel that me and my sister – especially my sister – are still picking up the tab for things that happened before the First World War. Doesn't that sound crazy? But I can't stop myself from thinking it. But then when I think of my life, the choice and the comfort I have, and then I think of her, I feel guilty. I mean, I'm sure my grandmother didn't want to be like that, I'm sure she didn't set out deliberately to terrorize three generations, it just happened that way. She had such a hard life – although of course, she never stopped telling us how hard it was for her, and how easy it was for us.'

He told me that his grandmother was a first-generation immigrant. She was born in Bergen, and in 1910, when she was sixteen, she migrated to the United States with her family. It was a classic migrant experience – travelling steerage, cardboard suitcases, possessions tied up in bundles. Through Ellis Island, like everybody else then, luggage labels tied to their coats. She said years later that she hated sentiment about that time, she said that it was awful, that if you hadn't been through it you couldn't imagine the coldness of it, the people checking you for vermin, treating you like you were nobody, nothing.

The family settled in the Mid-West, and although there was

already a large Scandinavian community there, the new migrants experienced hostility and prejudice. They were accused of being dirty, and to refute this, they overcompensated. 'My God,' Ted said, 'my grandmother was obsessed with dirt. You never saw a person like her – with the possible exception of my mom. My mother keeps the house so clean that you wouldn't believe it, you know, even things like the grill on the broiler or the lines between the tiles in the shower stall – I figure they're not supposed to be clean after a while. But not in our house. It was only when I went to college that I found out how fluff can gather in balls under the bed. It never got a chance to do that around Mom.'

To begin with, the new arrivals moved in with other members of the family who had moved to America some years earlier. For ten years, his grandmother worked in a boarding house there, doing laundry, cooking, washing down flights of stone steps, cleaning, cleaning, always cleaning things. Then she married 'the sweetest, most gentle guy you could ever hope to meet'. He worked with his family in running a general store, and so she started to work there instead, selling sugar and tea and cloth and wool, all sorts of things. She had a baby a year for the next ten years, but things being as they were, only six of them lived to adulthood. Ted's mother was her eldest daughter. By the end of the 1920s, things were better. The shop was doing well, and they felt that things were beginning to come together, when the Depression happened, 'and they were right back to square one'.

Ted said: 'One time I was in a supermarket with my mom, and I asked her, "Don't you think it's sort of obscene, there's just so much here, I mean *too* much of stuff like Twinkies and soda and junk like that?" But Mom stood there with a two-pound jar of mayonnaise in her hands and she said, "Believe me, if you'd gone through the Depression, you'd not think this obscene, you'd be glad you'd lived to see it." She put the mayonnaise in the cart, and I knew not to say anything else. And this you can't deny – my grandmother came through migration and marriage and the Depression and ten kids and the Second World War. I didn't. Maybe if she hadn't been so tough she wouldn't have made it through all those things.

'But she did everything she set out to do, and in the end, she had more than she could ever have dreamed of when she was young. The sad thing is, it didn't make her at all happy. Things picked up in later years and all her kids did well, they all got jobs and money. Dad was in Europe during the war, and when he came back, he and my mother got married. Then Dad went through college on the GI Bill, to become an engineer, while Mom helped support him, working as a secretary and running the house. In time Grammy saw Mom and all her kids with a good life style – nice big house in the suburbs, big car, smaller car that Mom took us to school in, me and my sister off to summer-camp every year. We were able to go to college, we didn't have to start working as young as she did. But it still wasn't enough.

'By the time she was an old lady, she was still lethal. The toughness that was there; I don't think that woman had a sentimental bone in her body. Do you believe this, Aisling? In all my life, I never once – not *once* – heard her say a nice thing to her daughter, my mother. Like, "You look pretty today," or "That dress looks good on you" – nothing. She made Mom just as tough as herself, and I think Mom supporting Dad ultimately had a bad effect. My mother could never stop being in charge after that. She had had to be super-capable from the time she was ten until Dad left college, so she wasn't going to stop then.

'Grammy lived with us in her last years, and I really do have to say, I think it was a relief to all of us when she died. My mom in particular was just burnt out from her. She was relieved, but she felt guilty about being so glad.

'There was an anger in Grammy, a rage. She fielded everything life threw at her, and yet I feel there was still a gap in the middle of her life, her self. There was something missing; she suspected that all along, and the older she got, the more she knew it, and the more she knew she'd never understand it, the madder she got. There was a part of her own soul that she'd never been able to come to terms with, and she just couldn't bear that – that all those years of being thrifty and hard-working and

God-fearing and clean hadn't been enough. That tormented her, that put her in a rage.

'I always think she lived too long, because she lived to see the sixties. It was as if society was suddenly discrediting all the things she'd done. She was so mad at my sister Amy. She was really into the sixties, she's older than me, and Grammy just couldn't bear it that she was protesting Vietnam and wearing strange clothes and living the way she did. My grandmother felt that after everything that had been done for her, Amy was just selling out. But I think Amy had to be the way she was, she couldn't just go on being like Grammy and Mom. The world changed too much. And I think my mother's shaping up to be just like her mother, that's what frightens me. After all those years of hard work and baking and taking us kids out to Trick or Treat at Hallowe'en, there's the same toughness, the same lack of something, the same anger building up.

'Amy's a mess by now. I mean she's done everything, she's done drugs, done alcohol, been in the hospital twice to dry out; she's divorced, she started her own business and it folded, she went back to waiting tables. She's mixed up, and she'd tell you as much. But what did my family expect? Did they want her to sell Girl Scout cookies and dress the tree once a year and buy two hundred dollar's worth of groceries once a week, and then everything would have been OK? In all the confusion, Amy's at least trying to find out what's missing at the centre of herself, and she admits that there is something missing, something wrong. Neither my grandmother nor my mother ever had the consciousness to know that about themselves. It's been awful, but I believe it's been inevitable, that there's some sort of crazy logic to it. I do think about my grandmother a lot. Compassion's important. Particularly when you don't understand, you have to try to be compassionate.'

He was quiet for a few moments, then he said, 'What about your grandmother, what was she like?'

I said, 'She was very tough too.'

The door of the church opened, and another tiny congregation came out, including the two women who had passed us earlier.

The bells of the church began to ring, and Ted looked at his watch. 'We'd better get going.' We went into the bar and paid for the coffee and cakes. The calendar behind the bar said that it was Sunday, the 29th of October, 1989. Within an hour the streets would be completely deserted. Already we could smell the odour of pasta sauces coming from high, open windows; from some, the clink of cutlery on plates could be heard. We squeezed past some cars parked absurdly tightly, and then suddenly Ted grabbed my arm.

'Look, Aisling, there's something I want to show you. Look up there, see what it says on that house over there? That's where Dostoyevsky finished writing *The Idiot*. Isn't that something?'

6

On the Monday after I had been to Florence, I called down with
Franca after lunch, to give her some sweets which I had brought
back for her. I found her in a bit of a temper, polishing the white
tiles of the hall by sliding up and down heavily with two thick
pads of felt strapped to her feet. She was pleased with the
sweets. She always liked to think she'd been remembered. There
was a real child in Franca. She went on polishing the floor as she
talked to me.

She had had a row with her daughter Lucia on Sunday. Lucia
had wanted to go to Rome with her friends to have a cup of
coffee, but Franca, usually indulgent, had put her foot down and
refused to be budged on the matter. It's over a two-hour drive
from S. Giorgio to Rome, which may seem like a stupidly long
way to go for a cup of coffee, but that's the whole point. It was
popular with the young people there to drive miles and miles for
some trivial reason – to Florence for a pizza, to the coast for an
ice-cream or a sandwich, or to spend half the night driving to a
disco in the next region. It's like the poor man's version of the
millionaire who flies to Paris to buy a box of chocolates, or to have
lunch – it's the grand gesture, not the thing itself that counts. For
once, Franca wore Lucia down, but it wasn't a total victory. They
had been invited to have lunch at Franca's old family home, in
the hills behind S. Giorgio. Lucia decided that if she wasn't going
to Rome, she wasn't going there either. They had a grand old
row, but in the end Lucia did stay in S. Giorgio. It was very
unusual for them to have a fight like this (partly because it was
very unusual for Franca to refuse Lucia anything). Lucia must

have been quite shocked by it. The following day, Monday, they were both still smarting.

I liked Lucia a lot. She was a source of great wonder to me, when I thought of myself at the same age. I remember being forced to live in a plum-coloured school uniform, studying until late into the night, conning the past historic of the verb 'to drink' in French, while listening to the storms coming in off the Atlantic. I used to see Lucia coming home from school. Sometimes I'd watch her walk across the square in a warm golden light with a couple of girls her own age, while I was out standing on the balcony. They sang softly together. The first time I heard it, I couldn't believe my ears, when I remembered the bus home from school in Ireland. Nobody sang sweet songs there; instead we all smoked and swore like a Black Maria full of lifers. Lucia had a Swatch with a blue sky and clouds on the face. All around the circumference, where the numbers should be, it said in French 'Life is not a valley of tears.' I wish I'd had a watch like that when I was fifteen.

Franca took the pads off her feet and brought me into the kitchen. She wanted to give me some of the cheese which her sister made, sheep's milk cheese.

'You must come up to the farm sometime,' she said as she wrapped up the cheese. 'I know you've been up into the hills, but you really will have to come with me. Come up at the end of the year, when they're killing the pig.' Lots of families in the country there fatten up a pig, and then in the middle of winter, the pig is slaughtered and butchered.

'Not to see the pig being killed, of course,' Franca added. 'That's not very nice to see. But it's interesting to see how they cut everything up, and make hams and salami and sausages. They say you can use every bit of the pig except its squeal. It's always a good day, always a good lunch to be had, a real *classico*.'

I said I'd like to go along.

'You can bring a friend too,' she said, grinning at me.

I said primly, 'Thanks.'

She put the packet of cheese on the table in front of me. 'You'll enjoy that. It's good, pure, real cheese. No additives or chemicals in that.'

There certainly weren't. Eating the cheese that night at dinner was the strangest sensation. I can only say that it was the oldest-tasting thing I have ever eaten. I could imagine shepherds in the hills eating such cheese hundreds of years ago, and it being exactly like that: the same sourish softness, oozing a little whey. It tasted as if there had been minimal human interference, as if it hadn't been made into cheese, but had simply been allowed to turn into cheese in its own time. The other things I ate that night, including a cake, a yoghurt and some bread, all tasted ersatz in comparison to the cheese.

It made me think of how we don't know the future, and we're forgetting the past. People in the past couldn't imagine the future in physical terms, because they didn't know the things there would be. We can't imagine the past because we can't forget the present, it clutters us out. The sense of the past that I got from the cheese interested me, because the future interests me, particularly the ability to read the future – not fortune telling, not pretending to know exactly what will happen. Nothing interests me less than astrology and all that mumbo-jumbo. But to know the spirit of the future is the important thing, and the people who can do that do it because they really understand the spirit of their own age. They aren't taken in by what seems to be the prevailing spirit of the times. Dostoyevsky could read the future in this way. It's one of the reasons I like his work so much.

When I was growing up in Ireland, I knew I wanted to leave, but I didn't know where I would go, I didn't know how it would be. I used to wonder what I'd be doing, and what I'd be like, when I was thirty. It was strange now to be in that future, which wasn't, of course, as I had imagined it. I suppose I had thought I would be happier, and again I thought of Lucia. It wasn't fair to compare me to her. It wasn't my fault, all the things that had happened. She didn't know what it was to grow up feeling dread in her own home, or what it was to fear someone everyone said she should love. I didn't want to think about where I would be after ten more years.

At the end of that week, Franca came to me, and asked would I do her a favour. She wanted to go to the ceremony in the cemetery for the Day of the Dead, but her mother-in-law wasn't well. She wanted me to go with her, and although I didn't really want to, I said that I would.

On the morning of the day, I met Franca downstairs. She was holding a pot full of bright yellow chrysanthemums, and a stout candle encased in red plastic. She had done a good trade in candles like this in the past week. Almost everyone bought them to place on or before the tombs of their families. It was a bitingly cold day. As it wasn't too far, we walked to the cemetery, which was beyond the town walls, on a slope at the back of S. Giorgio. It was old, and had become too small for the community. A new and bigger cemetery had been built down in the new part of S. Giorgio, for the people who lived there.

'*Che freddo!*' said Franca. Franca spent half the year saying how cold it was, and the rest of the time complaining about the heat. She took a few months at the transition from winter to spring and from summer to autumn to devote the full extent of her moaning to the effects of the change of the season, which she said gave her all sorts of allergies and aches and pains and moods. On this morning, though, I had to agree with her. It was no simple matter to stand outside in the cold for almost an hour. As we passed through the gates in the high walls, into the dimness of the cypress-shadowed cemetery, Franca commented, 'Look at all these old ladies. Don Antonio had better not keep us here any longer than he has to, or he'll have a few more dead bodies to pray over than he did at the start of Mass.' A few people turned to look at us disapprovingly as we giggled, and we did our best to look serious.

The Mass was to be said at a place which itself looked like one of the many mausoleums around the cemetery. It was a structure which consisted of a roof, three walls and a gate, which enclosed an altar. The gate, usually padlocked, had been opened, and a linen cloth and golden vessels had been set out. Don Antonio was just beginning to say Mass when Franca and I joined the huddle of women in front of the small chapel. I didn't concentrate much upon what was being said. I let my mind wander freely, but I tried to keep a look of complete distance and abstraction from my face – although I don't think anyone would have noticed.

I looked at Don Antonio as he fumbled through the motions. After all these years, it looked as if he too was trying not to let people see how much of a habit it had become to him, how little it meant to him. He also looked as if his mind were elsewhere, but maybe it just seemed that way. Maybe I was doing him a great injustice. He was so old. By the law of averages, he would soon be dead too, probably one of the first there to die. I wondered what it was like to know that you were at the end of your life. I was thirty then. I hadn't come round to the idea of death, of the inevitability of my own death. It wasn't something I cared to think about, I still held it to be an event that would be far in the future. I knew that to be too hung up on it would be a bad thing, because it would be a distraction from life. I had had more than enough of death in Ireland – not just personal bereavement, but the way it was in the air the whole time. People at home always seemed to be talking about who was dead, or just about to die, and they were always going to funerals. When I moved to France, I found it so strange. People must die in France as they do in Ireland, but it's more unobtrusive there. I was seventeen when my father died. I know that I was gossiped about because I didn't cry much, because I didn't seem to be particularly sad. I was gossiped about years later for exactly the opposite reason when my mother died, for crying too much. They said I felt guilty, and they said I deserved to, for having gone away and left my mother on her own. I didn't care what they said. I knew my own heart on these things, and that was what mattered. They hadn't had to live my life, they didn't know the things that had happened, they didn't know the complicated web of lies, secrets and violence there had been. I loved my parents after my own fashion, I can only suppose that they loved me after theirs.

Italian cemeteries are so different from graveyards at home. I like the place where my parents are buried; it's small and green and it overlooks the Atlantic. I found cemeteries eerie places in

Italy, too neat, too enclosed. I hate the dryness of them, the lack of soil. It's like being put away in a cupboard rather than being buried. I let my eyes wander around the place. Lots of the older tombs had photographs fused to them, on small ceramic ovals. The one nearest to me showed a man called Umberto Rossi, who died in 1936. The picture showed him, dark eyed and wearing a soft hat. Under the photograph were inscribed the words 'I know that I will rise again.' That suddenly struck me as being completely absurd. How could anyone ever think that he would live again, with his soft hat, this man from the past? It was all dust, whatever of the soul, the spirit. I couldn't believe that the body would rise: the idea of it repulsed me. What was I doing there?

They had reached the point in the Mass when the priest told them to put their flowers and candles before the graves, and then he started to sing a hymn in a wavering voice. The people joined in loudly as they lit the candles, and dispersed in the cemetery to put flowers and lights in front of the tombs of the people they had loved, their sons and wives and fathers and husbands and daughters. I thought it was the saddest thing, this remembrance. The power of human love can unsettle me, even though I know that there are only two things at the centre of life: the search for love, and the fact of death. Somebody gave Umberto Rossi flowers and wept for him.

Franca was tugging at my sleeve. It was only when she handed me a big white handkerchief that I realized I was crying too.

7

I often used to wonder if Adolfo, the waiter in the café that I used to go to in S. Giorgio, ever guessed that there was a reason for my early-morning visits, and what that reason was. Probably not. He never showed any signs of doing so. I only went there when I felt I had to. I would often call in of an evening, or after work, to sit on the spindly gilt chairs and read the papers there. But I never dropped in so early in the morning without my reason for doing so. Sometimes I would wake early at that period in my life, feeling very depressed, and then not be able to get back to sleep, so I would go to the bar to have a coffee and cake, and try to get myself ready to face the day. It usually helped to some degree.

It was barely seven when I went into the bar on that particular morning. I said hello to Adolfo and ordered a *cappuccino* and a *cornetto* with jam. I watched him as he made the coffee with a few deft movements, some bangs and hisses from the chrome coffee machine, and then the cup was set on the steel counter before me with a flourish. He flicked open the lid of the metal sugar container on the counter, and I helped myself, with the aid of one of the abnormally long spoons in it. Patting some chocolate powder on to the top of the milky foam he said, 'The cakes are arriving now,' and nodded towards the door.

A man was coming into the bar as he spoke, carrying on his shoulder a long shallow cardboard box, which he put down on the counter. Adolfo immediately started to lift the cakes from it, with rapid fluent movements of a pair of tongs, and to arrange them in the glass-fronted case directly under the counter.

'*Ecco!*' He had arrived at the *cornetti* and handed me one across the counter, wrapped in a small paper napkin. I took it, and continued to watch him while I ate, and drank my coffee.

Sometimes I would feel it was foolish to take not just such interest, but such solace, from this spectacle. There is something ridiculous about it, like buying yourself something small when you feel down, a bar of Swiss chocolate or some expensive soap, and absurdly feeling a bit better because of it. I pulled the *cornetto* apart. It was still warm and flaky because it was so fresh. It oozed apricot jam. I watched Adolfo as the man kept carrying in boxes of cakes, and carrying out empty ones when Adolfo had finished with them. The glass case quickly filled up with flat tarts full of yellow custard and scattered with crushed almonds; pies covered with heavily glazed fruit; rolls of apple strudel full of spice, sultanas and pine-nuts. The last box carried in contained savoury things, which were set in a space reserved for them on the left: crisp bread rolls with cheese and salami protruding from them; long savoury pastries full of smoked ham and egg. I admired the speed and neatness with which Adolfo emptied the boxes and filled the case, gently layering some of the flat cakes like tiles on a roof. I felt safe and contented to be there, in the warmth, with all the colours and the smells of the cakes. I felt as Hansel and Gretel must have done before they realized that the witch in the gingerbread house was going to eat them. Below the cakes there was a closed glass case, where there was a display of bottles of champagne, surrounded by paper streamers. Behind Adolfo there were glass shelves, laden with boxes of chocolates and expensive biscuits, together with glass jars filled with chocolate money, silver dragees, sugared almonds, and sweets wrapped in coloured foil.

The preceding afternoon, it had clouded over, and started to rain. It was seldom showery in S. Giorgio, and when the rain did begin, it could settle down without stopping for two days. This time it rained heavily, steadily, and I stood by the window looking out at it, until the apartment seemed to be totally enclosed by the weather, wrapped in greyness and darkness, and it triggered off in me a sense of desolation. Everything in my life – everything I valued and had struggled for, suddenly struck me as reprehensible. My independence, my job, my apartment, the books and music which meant so much to me, the whole external aspect I presented, all struck me as absurd. I thought of all the effort and energy I had expended and still needed to exercise every day to keep this whole show together, and it seemed pointless and foolish. I felt that I didn't have the energy to keep it all going. My life was fuelled by pure will. Nothing was left to chance, everything was willed, worked for, and yet it wasn't making me happy, it was just a new trap I had made for myself.

I felt my life beginning to unwind around me in a way that was no less terrible for it having happened many times before. I started to think of Ireland, of my family, my home; started to remember all the things I was trying to forget. I couldn't control my own mind, the old self-loathing, the familiar, bitter dissatisfaction with everything. The grey rain hammered down, driving in against the windows. I was too conscious of my self, of my own body, and I wanted desperately to flee myself, even if only for a short time. The rain was nailing me in, I felt as if I were in a cage. The rain sheeted across the square. It was too cold and dark to go out, and in any case, I was already too far gone, and where was there to go? I tried twice to call Ted but he wasn't there. On both occasions I could hear the phone ring and ring in the empty apartment. What good would it have done even if I had spoken to him? What difference would it have made, even if he had been there with me in S. Giorgio that night? When these fits of desolation came upon me, I felt completely isolated, irrevocably lonely, and to be with someone, particularly someone I liked, only made me more aware of how cut off I was from them, how isolated.

It wasn't other people who bothered me, it all came from inside myself, and the feeling was so strong that it was as if there were another person inside me, a dark self who tormented me. My self was split in two, and one half threatened the other, the weaker half.

And then, there in the apartment while the rain hammered

down, the strangest thing happened. I felt that this other self was no longer in me, but felt secure enough of her tight hold over me to risk slipping outside, to show me she was real and powerful. Now she was there in the room with me, standing behind me. I felt as you do when you go into an empty building, and you know that it's not really empty, that there is someone else there. You can sense their presence, even though you can't see or hear them. I thought that if I was to turn around, I would see her standing there right behind me, that other person. I could imagine that physically she would look completely unlike me, with an expression on her face somewhere between merriment and malice. 'But what's wrong with you? Frightened of your own shadow, just like you always were. Still a coward? Still frightened of your own self? What is there to be afraid of? Don't you know me? Don't you recognize me?'

The door bell rang. I didn't want to answer but it rang again. It was the bell immediately outside the apartment, at the top of the stairs, so I knew that it must be Franca or some of the family. I got up. The creature behind me melted away.

It was Lucia. She had borrowed a dictionary from me earlier that evening to do her English homework, and she had come to return it. As I spoke to her, I hoped that I was hiding efficiently what I was feeling. It was like someone who is held hostage in their own home, and is sent to the door to pay the milkman, but is warned not to tell him what is happening, or give any indication that something is wrong.

I looked at Lucia as if she were a being from another dimension. She seemed to me more unlikely than the person I had thought was standing behind me. I looked with wonder at her happy face, from which you could plainly see that she did not know torment, that she would never understand what it was to feel haunted. Her thick dark curls were pinned back with a plastic clip, with a white artificial flower attached to it. She was wearing jeans and a sweatshirt that said on it in English 'Winter Warmth', against a background of russet and orange leaves. There was a thin coloured Brazilian good-luck charm around her wrist, that some boy had given her, and which she always wore.

'Tutto bene, Aisling?'

I said that I was fine. She smiled and left.

I slept badly that night, and had terrible dreams. I often have nightmares, but even by my standards these were exceptional. Towards morning, I dreamt that I was combing my hair. My scalp was very itchy, and I didn't know why. Then I saw that impaled on the teeth of the comb were two big fat maggots, and I realized that the pain was coming from their gnawing my scalp. So I took a brush and brushed and brushed to get them out, and I did it so violently that my scalp was torn to pieces, my hair seeping with blood. And then I woke up.

I was in my room. It was still raining, it had rained all through the night. I looked at all the things around me – the clothes I had taken off the night before draped over a chair; a basket on the dressing table full of hairslides and bows; a long regular row of shoes; lipsticks and jars of face-cream and perfume bottles and hairbrushes. It struck me that I wouldn't be there for ever, and I wondered how I would ever find the energy to move. I thought it would be easier to just walk out of it some day and leave everything there, start all over again from scratch somewhere else. Then I remembered leaving Paris, and I knew that it couldn't be done, you couldn't slip out of your life like a snake shedding a skin. You could try, but at the end of the day, you'd still be the same person. It was myself that I wanted to get away from, and you can't do that just by abandoning a few pairs of shoes and some old cosmetics.

I made myself get up, and washed and dressed. It was still dark when I left the house, and walked through the narrow streets to the bar. In spite of the dream, in spite of having slept badly, I felt a bit better than I had done the night before. I was at a point when I felt it could be useful to go where there were other people, other things, where it was bright and warm and comforting, and where I could sit quietly for a while.

What was I going to do about this? I had already tried so hard. I had tried to be sensible, rational, told myself that I was depressed, that it was an illness like any other, and should be treated like any other.

The doctor I'd gone to see had a black leather bag with a long metal bar across the top and a complicated lock, the sort of bag that doctors were traditionally supposed to use to carry new babies to their parents. The doctor himself was staring at the bag while I spoke to him. He heard me out, and then gave a magnificent shrug.

'È la nostalgia,' he said, picking up his pen. 'Homesickness.'

The best thing to do, he said, would be for me to go back home to where I came from, back home to my *mamma*. I told him she was dead. He frowned, but went on writing and said that I should probably go back anyway. I could see he thought I was being unreasonable. If I went away from my own home, what could I expect, only unhappiness and loneliness? Until such time as I did return, he said, I could take these, and he handed me a prescription for some tranquillizers. I got them from the chemist, but I hardly ever used them. I didn't like the effect they had on me, and of course they didn't solve the problem. They couldn't make me feel less unhappy, just dulled, as if I had been hit on the head with something. Sometimes I was grateful for that.

So what was I to do? I still hoped that life itself would cure it. I thought that to go back to Ireland wouldn't help at all, because it was something that had been caused by my early life, it was a northern problem. I had tried to help myself as unhappy North Europeans had tried to help themselves for years: by going south. I wanted to believe that it had helped. It wasn't that the doctors of the south couldn't cure me – and of course they couldn't – but I couldn't be cured either by being close to what had hurt me in the first place.

I thought of the fresco of the man vomiting the devil. I thought of Don Antonio and his pendulum. If I had been living in some countries, I'd have been taken out to the edge of a wood, and left there, so that the dark things could come in the night and take away my evil. But I knew what caused my troubles. I had always known. The thing was, to try to change it. I had, I thought, spent all my adult life trying to work to that end, but on a night like last night it seemed to have all been in vain. I just didn't know what I should do instead.

I looked at my watch. I had to go home and get my things ready for work, or I'd be late. I said 'Ciao' to Adolfo, and he said, 'See you tomorrow.' I thought, 'I hope not,' as I walked out into the rain.

8

'This is the story: St Martin was riding along one day in winter, when he met a poor man who was begging by the side of the road. St Martin had no money to give as alms, so he took his cloak and he cut it in two, and he gave half of it to the poor man. And at that, the clouds suddenly rolled back, the sun shone, and it was warm. And ever since then, on the feast of St Martin, the 11th of November, the legend says that the weather will be unseasonably warm. It's called St Martin's Summer.'

Ted said that it must be true, for that day the sun had shone, and the sky had been clear. 'Of course,' I said, 'legends are always true, you must always believe them and take them seriously.' I told him that it was also called the Feast of Cuckolds, although I didn't know why. Italians love the idea of infidelity, they think it hilarious, particularly men being cheated on by their wives. They just like the *idea*, of course; they wouldn't like the fact of it happening to them any more than anyone else would. But it didn't surprise me that they had a feast for cuckolds. I just didn't understand why it should be associated with St Martin. If he was a saint, he was probably never married – saints never are – and even if he was, I don't think that it would be remembered in that way, I don't think he'd be held in esteem if he'd been betrayed by his wife.

There's a tradition, too, that on the feast of St Martin you drink the first of the new wine from that year's harvest, and eat roast chestnuts. That's what we were doing as I told him the story of the cloak. Ted had come down to S. Giorgio for the weekend, and Franca had given me a couple of bottles of very good new wine, from someone she knew who had a vineyard. She also gave me the loan of a pan in which to roast the chestnuts. Franca was one of the best people to know around S. Giorgio, because she knew everybody, and in Italy it's the private contact that opens doors. She was adept at getting the best of everything – wine, cheese, truffles, wild mushrooms, and she was always generous with me about such things. I think that she felt sorry for me in my ignorance when I arrived, and enjoyed watching me develop a taste and fondness for good wine and food. She knew that her gifts were appreciated and treated as they should be.

I opened the second bottle of wine so that it could breathe for a while until we were ready to drink it, and as I did that, I asked Ted to shake the pan over the fire, because I could smell the chestnuts burning. They smoked and rattled as he shook them gently. They had begun to swell a little, and you could see the white flesh showing through the cuts I had made in them earlier. They smelt good.

'More wine?'

'Yes, thanks.' He said that the wine was stronger than he had thought it would be.

'That's a mistake it's easy to make.' I said. 'Just because it's new wine doesn't mean that it's weak. Far from it. And because there isn't any label with information on it, there's no way of knowing how strong it will be. Look at this, it's still cloudy.' I held a bottle of new white wine to the light, so that Ted could see how turbid it was.

The room was quite hot from the fire, and we were listening to a record of Sibelius that I had recently bought. I liked my apartment very much, it could be very comfortable, especially at night. We didn't talk all the time. I never feel at ease with people if I can't sit in silence with them for long periods of time. He drank some wine, and I started to prepare the next batch of chestnuts, so that they would be ready to go on the fire when the first lot came off. One by one, I took them from the bag. They were big and fat and shiny, and one by one I cut a slit in them with a serrated knife. I like chores like that. I like the repetition and the slow rhythm of it. While I worked, I could feel that he

71

was watching me, and I wondered what he was thinking. I didn't ask.

The first batch of nuts was ready. I tipped them into a cloth, and put on the second lot, and all the time I could feel him looking at me. Suddenly, I realized how nervous I was. All the things that I thought were so well hidden – my own sense of desperation, all my terror – were things that he could see clearly, because he was looking at me in a way that people rarely did. He wasn't taken in by the manner I cultivated, he could easily see through that. He had listened to all the things I had said that day, and I now saw how long it was since that had happened, how rarely I had what could be termed a real conversation. You couldn't buy Ted over just by listening to him. One thing I learnt early in life is that people love to talk about themselves, and you can easily use this to deflect attention from yourself, if you so desire. I had noticed this most particularly with Fabiola. She could happily walk away from me (and no doubt from many other people too), thinking she had just had a conversation about marriage or families or holidays, without realizing that it had been a monologue, to which I had made no contribution whatsoever. I could even stay completely silent, it wasn't necessary to nod my head and say 'Yes,' or 'How true,' or anything at all, it was simply enough that I was there. Franca was more shrewd, but after all the years I had been there, she took me according to her own lights. She didn't see me as others did, didn't accept the image I projected, but had her own version of my strangeness which was closer to the truth, but still not the whole picture. So it really unnerved me to be with someone who was determined to get beyond the smoke screen, and to know me. I kneaded the cloth with the chestnuts in it too much. They don't need that much pressure to loosen the skins, and I realized that I had been mashing them relentlessly for some time now. I unrolled the cloth and offered them to him. The chestnuts held the heat of the fire in them, and were hard to hold. He topped up my wineglass. I was drinking a lot out of nervousness.

'Isn't it nice all these traditions they have here in Italy? I've never seen another country like it in that respect, there seems to be no end of festivals and celebrations.'

Ted said that he had never taken much interest in things like that up until then. Even Thanksgiving and Christmas didn't mean much to him, he told me that he would have been quite happy to spend them alone. 'Because I work with Americans, we usually do get together at Thanksgiving and have a turkey dinner. Last year one of my students asked me why it was Italians never celebrated Thanksgiving. I told him to think real hard about why *we* celebrate it. No, I guess it is fun to get together, but if we didn't, I could do without it.'

I said that I thought that was a pity. 'Those things are so lovely. You need little celebrations in life. If you took away all those things, life would be grey. There'd be nothing left but necessity. I bet you haven't had a birthday cake since you were small.' He said that he hadn't.

'It shouldn't be like that. Life's hard enough. When I asked Franca could I borrow the pan for the chestnuts because I had a friend coming to see me, she asked, "Is he Italian?" When I said, "No, American," she handed it over at once and sighed and said, "Ah, these poor Americans. We have to do what we can for them, because they have nothing of their own, no food worth talking about, no festivals, no fun!"'

'America isn't that bad!'

'Franca thinks it must be. She's always shaking her head and saying "*Questi poveri Americani.*" She said to me once, "You know, Aisling, it's much worse for the Americans than it is for the Germans. They at least can get on a train, or get in a car and drive down to Italy. America's so far away."'

'Has she ever been there?'

'Franca? Are you kidding?'

Ted shook his head, and said that that was always the way. People were always sounding off about the States, but if you asked them, you usually found that they hadn't been there at all, that they were going on nothing more than a few loud-mouthed tourists, and some of the worst television. He said that people should visit the country before they judged it. Parts of it were really horrible, he admitted, and he was glad that he wasn't living there any more. But there were, he said, great things about it. Even apart from whether you liked it or not, he felt that it was good to see America because 'it has such a big influence on the rest of the world that it's worth going there just to check it out.'

'I'd like to visit America,' I said. 'Do you know the part of the autostrada here just after you join it, near the lower part of S. Giorgio? The road we were on this afternoon? That always makes me think "This is what the States must be like." That big wide road, and all along the side of it all those factories, including the place where I work. They're all flood-lit at night, and there are huge signs with the names of the firms on them. There's even a motel, with its name in English – The Maple-Leaf Motel. The scale is inhuman, you can't walk anywhere around there, you can only get to those places by car. I can't imagine anyone could ever feel a sense of fondness or belonging for a place like that. I sometimes think that a lot of America must look and feel like that part of the autostrada. But I could be wrong.'

'Listen, Aisling,' Ted said suddenly excited. 'I'm probably going home for a week or two in the spring. You should come with me, just for a vacation. It would be a good opportunity for you to see the States. And I'd really enjoy your being there.'

'If I can afford it, and can get the time off work, I'd love to.'

'Then maybe we could do it the other way around, and the next time you go to Ireland, I could go with you.'

I laughed and said, 'You're still mad keen to get there, aren't you? Maybe we will do that sometime. Franca is always saying to me, "Never say never, Aisling." I don't have any plans to go in the immediate future, but who knows? If I was going there, it would be nice to go with you. Sometimes I think I would like to go back, more than I used to.'

Then I remembered that there was something I wanted to tell him. 'The loveliest thing happened this week, Ted, on Tuesday afternoon.' I had just got back from work, and I saw a dark shape over on the window sill. I saw that it was a bird, which was odd enough in itself, for the hunters had killed or driven away almost all the birds locally. But this was too big to be a sparrow or a finch, and when I went over, very quietly so as not to disturb it, I saw that it was a young owl. It had a thick feathery neck, and round yellow eyes, which disappeared into black slits when it blinked. It looked in at me, but without seeming to see me, then it turned its head and looked out over the roofs of the town. It had big clawed feet, which looked out of proportion to the rest of its body. Its claws and its eyes made you know it was a predator. The most sentimental person couldn't have thought it was cute, for all its soft feathers and its littleness. I liked it for that, for its otherness, its pride. It was a thing you had to respect. It stayed there for about half an hour, sometimes looking blankly through the window, sometimes sitting with its eyes closed for periods of time. And then, at last, it spread its wings and flew away.

I told Ted that all the time, it became more and more important for me to see things like that – not just pleasant, but important, or even just to know that they existed. Sometimes I like to think about seals swimming in the ocean, or of a whale rising out at sea. I like the timelessness of nature, of animals. If you see a seal, it looks as it would have looked had you seen it a hundred, a thousand years ago. I like the otherness, the completeness of animals. Sometimes, I told him, when I'm feeling really down, I like to think about animals and how they live. It makes me feel that there is some beauty and mystery left, something other than the way I live.

I could sense the question that was going to follow: And what makes you so unhappy, Aisling? He didn't say it, but he was looking at me very hard, and I knew that he was going to ask. I rattled on nervously, so that he wouldn't have a chance to speak.

'I even like going to the zoo. I know that's bad. In principle I don't agree with it, but a part of me can't resist it, because I see animals there I would never see anywhere else. I can hardly believe how strange and beautiful they are. The best thing of all is that they're alive. They're not like a painting, or a thing that's been made. The more you know about them, the more amazing they are. You wouldn't believe some of the ways they're adapted to their environment, like polar bears have hollow fur. Did you know that? It keeps them much warmer than it would if it wasn't hollow. I have all these books, see,' I pointed to the shelves, 'books about animals, and plants too. We think we know it all, but we don't know anything. I'd like to have some animals of my own. I can't have any here, Franca won't allow me, but some day I will. A Persian cat and a cockatoo. That's what I'd like.'

I had started to cry just after I began to rattle on crazily in this way, and in the middle of it, I had gone over to the shelf and pulled out some books, as if that would prove my point. Suddenly I saw myself as he saw me, and it was like waking out of a dream. I was sitting there by the fire, surrounded by shards of broken chestnut shells, which I had spilled from my lap when I stood up. There were a few coffee-table books on the rug – *Plants and Animals of the Amazon Rainforest*, *The Great Barrier Reef in Pictures*. I was sitting in the middle of all this clutter, crying, and I could see the bewildered look on his face. Suddenly, I screamed defiantly at him, 'I could kill someone, I really could! Myself or someone else, it makes no difference, just don't think I couldn't!'

He didn't say anything. He went on looking at me with a sort of fearless amazement, as if he didn't know how to react, and then he held his hand out to me and said very softly, 'Hey honey, who ever said you couldn't?'

I put my arm up across my face as if to ward off a blow, a blow which was not struck. He put his arm around me, and I wept as I hadn't allowed another person to see me do for years and years.

It meant so much to me to have him there, and I told him so. If he hadn't been there that night, I would probably have been down with Franca and her family. They were very good to me. Sometimes I appreciated being in the company of other people for a while. I could imagine the scene downstairs on a Saturday night. The whole family would be sitting around the TV, watching some endless variety show, with singers, a lit-up staircase, ugly middle-aged male compères, and lots of young women in skimpy costumes flitting about, sexy in the way an inflatable doll is sexy. I would be sitting by the fire. Franca would be moaning about Davide (while giving him the odd poke with her toe), or about work or Lucia or the people in the village, or whatever, but a large part of my mind would have been locked

76

into my own thoughts. I'd have drunk too much, and then late at night I'd have thanked them and come back up to my own cold apartment, the hearth dead, the whole place empty and dark.

'Today was fun, wasn't it?' Ted said. 'I liked that a lot. We should do it again, we can go to all sorts of places together, go to the sea, go anywhere you want.'

'Today was lovely.'

We had gone to visit another hill village in the area, smaller and higher in situation than S. Giorgio. We had driven there in my car, out along quiet roads, and the dark fertile land was beautiful. The twisted vines were bare, and even at this, the bleakest season of the year, the richness of the land was clear to see. The road wound up into the hills, we parked outside the town walls, and looked out over the valley. We could see for ever so far, back across the plain, back to S. Giorgio itself, spilling down the side of a distant hill. The whole scene was washed by an unexpected bright pink light, of the sun late on a winter afternoon. The streets of the town were almost empty; our footsteps echoed loudly. In the church there was a fresco, and the background of it showed exactly the local landscape: the same slender trees, the same all-pervasive softness, the same pearly light. The steep streets of the town were cobbled. A hefty cat sat on the wall which surrounded a small garden; the garden as empty and still as an ornament under glass. The heaped clouds were all pink.

The day had been special to me because it had been so ordinary. We hadn't done anything in particular, and there were so many similar pretty towns around we could have visited. More and more I had come to treasure the ordinary things of life, and to feel ill at ease with things that proclaim their strangeness, their exclusivity. First-class hotels and smart restaurants unnerve me, not least because I feel that they were planned to unnerve people. Functional things have much more warmth and appeal. And sometimes an ordinary, happy situation can be so hard to find, that when it does happen, when you find yourself in a quiet town on a winter afternoon with someone you like, it doesn't seem ordinary any more, it seems miraculous.

77

We didn't speak for a while. I let the silence run on, took the chestnuts from the fire, poured out more wine, and still he said nothing. I asked him if he was afraid of me, and he didn't answer immediately.

'Yes, sometimes I am. I admit that. Maybe a bit less so now. I think I'm beginning to understand you a bit better, and I like you a lot. But you never took me in, though, not even at the start. Do you remember the weekend you came up to see me in Florence, and we met a friend of mine at the station when I was seeing you off?' I remembered him, remembered how he had grinned and stared at me, the way people look at their friends' new lovers. I had been my most charming self. 'That guy teaches with me. I met him in the college a couple of days later, and he said, "That Irish girl I met you with at the station on Sunday night seems like a real sweetie." And I thought to myself "Oh yeah?" I could see why he thought that, but I know the score. I know you might not like me saying this, Aisling, in fact I know you don't want pity, but I have to say it – sometimes I feel real sorry for you.'

'Yeah, well, thanks,' I mumbled. 'Saves me the bother of feeling sorry for myself. Things change, though, don't they, Ted? Some people hate change, they want life always to stay the same, even if it isn't up to anything much. But for me, I always like to know that things can be different, even that they're bound to be different in time. Sometimes people tell you they want to change their lives, but if the opportunity to do that presents itself, they just shy away. I always try to be vigilant with myself in that way, I try to be sure that I'm not fooling myself. But it's hard to make changes happen. Sheer will isn't enough. I know that now.'

'I like you. There are lots of things I like about you. I just wish you liked yourself a bit more.'

I suspected that it was Ted who was the sweetie. He couldn't imagine that life could feel like a winter night, when you walk along a wet street, and you see all the lights and fires in the houses, and you recognize all the faces of the people inside. But if you ask at any door, there's always a plausible reason, not unkindly meant, as to why you can't come in. I remember very clearly those two days when Ted came to stay with me, and I think everyone remembers the weekend of 11th November, 1989, when the Germans opened the Berlin Wall, just as everyone remembers where they were during that whole autumn, when things were changing so fast all over Eastern Europe. It was one of those times like when someone else has a baby, and you can afford to be delighted because you're not the one who's going to be changing its nappies or seeing to it when it cries in the middle of the night. A wall across a city is so self-evidently a bad thing that when it came down it was easy to feel a simplistic pleasure, and just enjoy the pictures of people dancing on the Brandenburg monument or Rostropovich giving a concert beside the wall, or young women giving roses to the soldiers and all that. You could console yourself with the thought that it was the end of something bad, without bothering yourself too much about whether it was the start of something good. It was like taking a wedding at face value and confusing it with the marriage to come. Life gives so few opportunities for easy optimism, that when such an occasion presents itself, it's hard to resist.

On the Sunday morning, Ted went out to get the newspapers while I put on the coffee. While I was waiting for it, I went out on to the kitchen balcony, which overlooked the square. There were two balconies in the apartment in S. Giorgio. The other was in the bedroom, and overlooked the yard at the back of the shop. It was a singularly unpicturesque view. The yard was full of old crates and stuff, and there were also a couple of brokendown Fiat 500s. They were good little cars, so good that they went out of production. Franca had a 500, and had bought the old wrecks in the yard to raid for spare parts, as there was no other way of getting them. Beyond the yard were the backs of some other apartments, many of which could have done with a lick of paint. These buildings also had balconies, and there were usually a few frames of laundry sitting out on them to dry. I actually liked both views, and thought that they complemented each other very well. From the kitchen you could see S. Giorgio as the tourist board wanted you to see it – pretty, quaint, with the church and the café and the little shops full of pottery. Then if you went into the bedroom, you could see another aspect of the town, one less well publicized – its dreariness, its provinciality. I liked the view from the bedroom, because while you can see pictures of the pretty side of Italy, even of S. Giorgio, while you're still abroad, you'll only ever see such dreariness if you go to the place itself. It's why I sometimes think you can get more of a sense of a country which you haven't yet visited from a batch of badly taken holiday photographs than from a glossy coffee-table book which shows only the most beautiful places, looking better than they could ever do in real life. It gives such a false impression. There are places in Tuscany and Umbria and until you've seen them for yourself you wouldn't believe how drab and dreary they can be.

I watched Ted from the balcony as he walked across the crowded square. I always like watching people I know from a distance, I don't know why, it makes me feel powerful. I recognized quite a few of the people down in the square that morning, and I scrutinized them after Ted had vanished into the paper shop. Sunday morning is always busy in S. Giorgio, summer and winter. Suddenly I spotted Fabiola and her husband Pietro, who was carrying their baby in his arms. Fabiola was wearing a mink jacket, and the baby was hopelessly overdressed in a velvet cape with a white collar, white hat, and clumpy black shoes. They had just come out of a cake shop, and Fabiola was holding a flat package, wrapped in red paper and tied with a yellow bow. The loose ends of the ribbon had been carefully coiled into long springy ringlets.

I often saw Fabiola and Pietro like this on a Sunday morning: Pietro's mother lived in S. Giorgio, and they usually had Sunday lunch with her. The scene was repeated all over the square: expensive cars were being parked, the man always in the driver's seat, the woman in furs, or an elegant suit, their child (there was rarely more than one) stiflingly overdressed. I stared down at Fabiola with rapt attention, as if my look could pierce the veneer of her life. She was smiling broadly and blankly. She knew that everyone in S. Giorgio knew her; knew too that she was the loveliest, the most elegantly dressed, and the most affluent woman in the square at that moment. That was the source of her power. Hers was a life of pure surface, and she felt no pain, because there was nothing inside to be hurt. Her greatest contentment came from the knowledge that others could only aspire to the life she had. That the things she had ultimately bored her was of no importance. The people who coveted her possessions – her jewels, her cars, her money – did not know this, and imagined they must surely make Fabiola happy, and would make them happy too, if they were in her place. Her happiness came instead from being the focus of this envy. Peering down at her, I wished that I could take everything away from her, if only for a moment – her furs, her jewellery, her house, all her make-up and smart clothes, even her husband and child. More than that, I wanted to deny her the right to partake in all these rigidly fixed social conventions – her presence in the square on Sunday, the family lunch, even the obligatory wrapped cake. I wanted to take all these things away, because I wanted to know if, stripped of her possessions and her social context, there would be anything there at all. I doubted it: not even a naked, shivering scrap of suffering humanity would remain.

Suddenly, everything went black. Someone had crept out on to the balcony behind me, and was pressing their hands tightly over my eyes. I screamed and lashed out violently. At once I was free again, and there was a loud crash as the person behind me fell backwards over a potted plant into the apartment. Everybody down in the square heard both the scream and the crash, and were now staring up at me, including, to my mortification, Pietro and Fabiola. I stepped quickly back into the kitchen, and slammed the balcony doors.

Ted picked himself up off the kitchen floor, rubbing his head. 'Jesus, it was only a joke!' I said angrily that I hadn't found it a very funny one, and that I was surprised at his being so insensitive. Then I saw it from his point of view. I said I was sorry and I started to cry. He put his arm around me and said he was sorry too, that it was a stupid thing to have done, and then I started to laugh, because I was in that nervous state when there's

81

hardly any difference between laughing and crying. But I felt afraid that having let him see how vulnerable I was the night before, I'd never be able to hide my nervousness from him again. And while part of me was relieved by this, part of me was appalled.

9

The day after Ted went back up to Florence, I had a letter from my brother Jimmy in Dublin. I can't say I was altogether pleased when I opened the post-box and saw it sitting there. I never got on particularly well with Jimmy. At best we had nothing much in common, at worst we fought dirty and vicious to hurt each other in the way only siblings can. I always do a double take when I see a letter from Jimmy, because his handwriting is exactly the same as mine. He also talks like me, and moves like me; we have all the same little mannerisms. If you saw a photo of me and a photo of Jimmy, you wouldn't say that we look alike at all, but if you saw us together, in real life, you'd know immediately that we were brother and sister.

I had just arrived home from work. Usually I rip open my post and read it on my way up the stairs, but I took this particular letter up to the apartment intact. I was looking forward to lunch, and I was afraid that Jimmy's letter might spoil it for me if I read it first. While I was cooking and eating, however, I couldn't stop thinking about him.

I thought it was really unfair that although Jimmy had given my mother far more trouble and cause for worry than I ever had, at the end of her life he was seen as the good son, and I was cast as the selfish and irresponsible one, The Girl Who Broke Her Mother's Heart. Jimmy's six years older than I am. When he was eighteen, he took himself off to London and lived in a squat there. We hardly ever heard from him, and when we did, it was never good news. My mother used to cry about him, and there was nobody locally with whom she could share her woes, because she was so ashamed. She invented some elaborate story about how he had a job in London and how well he was doing over there. I remember how people used to stop us coming out of Mass on a Sunday morning, and if they asked after Jimmy my mother would tell them the most blatant lies so artlessly that for a time I was completely confused, and wondered if he really was working in England, and for reasons of her own, she pretended in the house that he had gone to the dogs. She used to complain bitterly on the way home from chapel, and say that on top of everything, Jimmy was guilty of 'making me sin my soul coming straight from the altar rails'. That in itself was another lie, of course. Later I came to appreciate that my mother was a born liar, that there was a layer of deceit and a facility for fabrication in her that I have seldom seen surpassed. It seemed an extraordinary aberration, because outwardly she was such a pious person, but I came later to see that piety and deceit were not mutually exclusive, as you might imagine. She was also adept at self-delusion, and cherished double standards. Years later, when Jimmy was home again and back in her good books, she remarked casually one day, 'I never was really that worried, Aisling, and anyway, what sort of a man is it who doesn't sow his wild oats?'

When he was in England, there was even a period when she wanted to go over and find him, and make him come home, but my father wouldn't let her go, and he was right. My mother knew nothing of city life: a trip to Dublin every year on the 8th of December to do a bit of Christmas shopping was as much as she knew, and almost more than she could handle. I can hardly bear even now to imagine her wandering around in the Underground, looking for Jimmy.

He was arrested and charged once for possession of drugs – a bit of marijuana – and once he crashed his motorbike near Brighton and broke his leg. To be honest, I thought that for a black sheep in a family in the mid 1970s he wasn't up to much, and I told him so. He was really angry with me.

He didn't stay in London very long – I think it was just about a year and a half altogether, and then he came back to Ireland and reverted to being completely conservative and conventional. By various contacts he managed to get a job in an insurance company in Dublin, and soon my mother didn't have to tell lies about him to the neighbours any more. He bought a car, and came home to see us most weekends. There was a woman called Nuala who worked in the same office, and she was also from Clare. Jimmy used to give her a lift home as far as Ballyvaughan when he was going home, and a year or so after they first met, they got engaged.

If I didn't have much in common with Jimmy, I had absolutely nothing in common with Nuala. Thinking about it from the safe distance of S. Giorgio, however, I could see how I cultivated the differences, even if only in my own mind, because I was so afraid of being like her. We were from very similar homes in the same part of Ireland, and I think she was the sort of woman my mother would have been had she been born later. It therefore follows that Nuala was the sort of woman my mother would have liked *me* to be; and that Jimmy was marrying her because she was like my mother. In some ways families appear to be such a complex web of emotions and psychology, but if you look at it carefully, it's often frighteningly simple. People marry people like their parents. After eighteen years with my father, however, I made a conscious choice that I would never marry a man like him. The catch was, I thought that all men were like my father, even the ones who seemed to be nice, they were only pretending until such time as they had you in their clutches, and then they would let all their nasty side out, and there would be nothing you could do about it. As I got a bit older, in my early twenties, I suspected that this wasn't the whole story, but I was still frightened. Then I went to Paris and I met Bill and I felt at first that he was concrete evidence that my earlier theory was false. Then he left me, and I swung right in the other direction, and thought that this was a classic proof of what I had believed when I was a girl. There's something particularly galling about knowing that you had more savvy about men and the ways of the world when you were fourteen than when you were twenty-four. It seemed strange to me now at thirty to have gone through all this and to know what I did, and yet still to be so baffled.

85

Anyhow, my relationship with my family began to sour a bit around the time Nuala and Jimmy got married. Our father was dead by then. Inevitably, the wedding itself was a source of dissent. Nuala was going for clear soup, turkey and ham, a three-piece band, and seventy guests in a hotel in Ballyvaughan; it was to be your standard Irish wedding. I am not, however, your standard Irish bridesmaid, but Nuala couldn't see that, and for some reason she thought that her day wouldn't be complete if I didn't go up the aisle behind her in some ridiculous yellow tulle confection. I refused politely, but she persisted until I refused rudely, and then of course I got terrible flak from my mother and Jimmy.

Jimmy and Nuala were married in spring, and I went up to Dublin to go to university that autumn. To my amazement, everyone took it for granted that I would lodge with them in their new house. That didn't fit in with my plans at all. For years I had been slogging away at school so that I could get to university and be independent in the city, and I wasn't going to let that slip from me now. My mother said that it would be such a help to them with their mortgage; I replied that their mortgage was no concern of mine, and if they needed help they could always get a lodger, it didn't have to be me. I guessed, correctly, that they would probably have a baby within a year, and that if I was living with them, I would get roped in for unpaid babysitting. Nuala and Jimmy still went up and down to Clare most weekends, but I seldom accepted their offer of a lift. I preferred to stay in the city, and for this they said I was selfish and had abandoned my mother. It wasn't fair: I wrote to her and phoned her very often, but I have to admit, I was ruthless about claiming my own life, and still feel I was right to do so.

What I resented most of all was the implication that I was up to something nefarious in my tatty little bedsit in Ranelagh, engaged in things which would never have been tolerated in a respectable home like Jimmy's and Nuala's. In fact, I was leading a completely innocuous life, and my new pleasures were touch-ingly simple: cooking and eating what I wanted when I wanted;

listening to Bartok until all hours on an old stereo I had bought myself second hand, eating a few chocolates out of a box and then going out, secure in the knowledge that when I came home, the Raspberry Whirl would still be there. That first year in the city was one of the happiest times in my life.

People get so defensive when they get into their late twenties or early thirties, when they begin to make big choices in life. If they get married then they seem to think that you should be married too, or if they buy a house, they see an implicit criticism in the fact that you're still renting. I used to feel that sort of pressure a lot with Nuala and Jimmy, and when I left Ireland, I think they took it personally. I haven't got this particular hang-up myself (one of the few I seemed to have missed out on). I don't think other people should do what I'm doing just because I'm doing it. I'd have been appalled if Jimmy and Nuala had followed me to Paris.

Yet the strangest thing of all is that I love Jimmy, and I know that he loves me. I suppose that if, instead of a letter, he'd been right there with me in S. Giorgio, we'd have been scoring points off each other the way we always did. And yet I'd lay down my life for Jimmy, and I know he'd do the same for me. I don't use the word 'love' lightly, and my love is hard to engage. It's a mysterious thing. People generally don't like to admit that you can love people you don't like, but you can. It's not ideal, in fact it's confusing and painful, but I suspect that it happens a lot. That's why unhappy families can hold together for years and years. You can even love people who are cruel to you, and so there are women who love violent men. And a terrible lie grew out of this – that it's the violence they love, and not the person who inflicts it. Such women love these men *in spite of* the cruelty, never because of it.

Of course, the world would be a better place if liking and loving went together. Life would be simpler, and hideous myths, like the one I've just mentioned, would have no credence whatsoever. But it's never an easy thing to bear. I know what it's like. It's best if you like the people you love, and I wish I liked Jimmy more, wish I had liked my parents more, although I don't blame myself for not doing so. I had the best possible reason for not liking my father.

I had finished eating my lunch, but I decided I'd wash up, and then read the letter over a cup of coffee. As I cleared things away and filled the sink with hot water, I thought of how there was something unusual in the relationship between Jimmy and me. Usually when there's an age gap of six years it makes a big difference when you're small and is less important when you're adults. But with us it worked the other way round: we were good chums when we were children, but grew apart when we grew up.

Our family home was in an isolated part of the country, and because there were no other children around, we were thrown into each other's company. The age difference worked well for both of us. It meant that when Jimmy was twelve, he could play childish games with me without loss of face, when he was just that bit too old for them, but still wasn't ready to give them up. For me, the bonus was that Jimmy was so good at everything because he was bigger. He could draw well, and do complicated jigsaws and he was brilliant at making things. When I was eight, for example, he made a car out of cardboard boxes for my two favourite dolls. It was exactly the right size for them, and it had windows and wheels and everything, even two headlights that really worked. (They were actually two pocket-torches.)

As I wiped the plates, I was surprised by how many pleasant memories came back to me. When I was six, I wanted a cat more than anything else in the whole world. I used to pray every night that God would send me a cat, and then one day, Jimmy came home from school with a kitten sitting in a box full of straw. One of his friends' cats had had a litter, and he had asked for one when it was big enough. My parents had never given in to my pleading, but Jimmy knew that if he just showed up at the house with a kitten in a box that he'd probably be able to coax my parents round.

He was right: I was allowed to keep the kitten. I can still see that cat sitting in its box, as if it was yesterday. I can still see it struggling to its feet on the straw, and opening its pink, frail mouth. It was a female cat, so I called her Nora. She was a black cat with white socks and a white splodge on her face. I loved Nora so much, and I looked after her for years. And then when I was about twelve, my father killed her one night after he'd been drinking. The next day he said it was an accident, and my mother said Nora was an old cat, and maybe she had been going to die anyway, but I didn't believe either of them.

Another time, when I was about eight, there was a carnival on near our home, and Jimmy took me there with his friends. There was a stall where you threw darts at little badges pinned to squares of cardboard, and if your dart hit the card, you won. Jimmy and his friends played darts for almost the whole evening, and they gave me all the badges they won. When I went home that night, from neck to waist my coat was completely covered with coloured badges. It was a great feeling.

Waiting for the coffee, I remembered a day when Jimmy and I went out for a walk, and I got tired on the way back. I got slower and slower until I came to a complete halt, and Jimmy had to give me a piggyback home. I loved that, loved being so high off the ground. I buried my face in the back of his neck, and closed my eyes, then pretended to myself that I was really riding a pony. And then I fell asleep. When I woke up we were in a dark lane, with trees on either side of it. I held on tightly to Jimmy, and flung back my head. It was spring, and the trees were covered in blossom, wild apple, wild cherry. There was a wind, and the wind blew the petals from the trees, and the sunlight was broken by the branches of the trees. I remember feeling mad with happiness, and I wished that we would never go home again, that Jimmy would carry me through the fields and the hills for ever.

There was nothing else for it now. I lifted the letter down from the shelf where I had earlier propped it against a bottle of wine, and ripped it open.

Hello Aisling,
Well, the letters are few and far between, yours and mine both, so you know how it is. It's hard to find the time and energy

after a day's work, so I keep putting it off, and putting it off. I said I'd do it this weekend, and it's now ten o'clock on Sunday night, so I suppose if I don't write now, before I sleep, I'll never do it.

Anyway, the main reason I want to write is that I have a bit of news for you. Nuala's expecting another baby next May. We're both really happy about it, and Sinead and Michael are all excited about having a new brother or sister. This'll be the last time. Three's enough – enough for us, anyway. As it was, the house here was getting too small for us, and we were planning to move. The kids are getting bigger, and soon Sinead'll need a room of her own. So we'd just put a deposit on a house in Chapelizod – a new house, in one of those new developments that are going up all over the place now, and then we found out there was another baby on the way. So it's all working out well. We're trying to sell this place at the minute. We'll be moving early next year, if all goes well.

I'm doing OK in work. Got promoted a while back. It means a bit of extra money which is always useful, but particularly so now. I suppose sometimes I do worry a bit about money, but what can you do? I don't want Nuala to even think of going back to work: maybe in a few years' time, when all the kids are bigger and at school. We've managed OK so far. Nuala's a real good mother and a good housewife. She knows how to make whatever money we have go as far as possible, and we have lots of baby things left over from Sinead and Michael, so that should be a saving.

Anyway, I'm sure all of this is boring you. How are you, Aisling? Do you ever think of coming back? I mean, for a holiday. If you'd like to come for Christmas you know you'd be very welcome, or if you come next summer, you could see the new baby and the new house. We'll have more room to put you up there, but there's always room for you here.

I know the kids would love to see you. Sinead's old enough now to understand about her aunt being in Italy and where Italy is, and that they speak a different language there and all that. She's a great kid. She reminds me a bit of you when you were that age, although she doesn't look like you. She looks like Nuala. Michael looks like me.

We still go back home to Clare some weekends. It's great having the house there for the holidays. It's a real saving, and the kids love it. I'd like to take Nuala away sometime on her own for a real holiday, to Spain or somewhere like that. I know she'd love it. Well, maybe someday.

Anyway, that's everything. I'll finish up here. Tomorrow's Monday morning, back to the grindstone, you know, so I'd better get a good night's sleep. Nuala was asking for you. The kids send their love. I hope you're OK. Drop us a line sometime.
Your fond brother,
Jimmy

Well, you'd have to have seen other letters from Jimmy to appreciate the difference between them and this one. This letter wasn't an olive branch, it was a complete olive tree. When Jimmy wrote, he always asked if I was coming home, but it would be framed more along the lines of, 'I don't suppose there's much chance of your taking the trouble to grace us with your presence this summer, I'm sure there are far more exotic places in Italy where you'd rather go.' Then I'd write back something like 'You bet, who wants to spend their time in Glasnevin when they could be in Lucca,' and then I wouldn't hear from him again for months.

I quickly read over the letter again. There was a sort of heroic ordinariness to Jimmy's life now that I admired so much. 'I suppose sometimes I do worry a bit about money, but what can you do?' I imagined the reality behind that, imagined Jimmy lying awake at night beside Nuala, doing endless calculations in his head, which never worked out exactly as he would have wanted them to. He was utterly steeped in suburban domesticity, which in one way was a very straightforward way of life. You could see it mapped out before you for thirty years; though in other ways it was an endless struggle. But what I noticed most of all in the letter was that Jimmy sounded happy. There was the odd wistful overtone, but generally he sounded like a man who had made the right choice for himself in life and was contented with it. He must have mellowed considerably, as he had enough goodwill left over to extend a little to me. I could see how cautious he was, afraid that I was as prickly and difficult as ever.

And maybe I was. I wouldn't go home for Christmas. It was too late now anyway, it would be hard to get a flight, and in any case, I had already made plans with Ted for Christmas. But the real reason was that I knew I wouldn't like Christmas with them, that their way of life wasn't for me, and it might do more harm than good. I was keen to build on the goodwill Jimmy tentatively offered in the letter, and it made me sad to think that it was still best to do that from a distance. I was the one at fault here, not Jimmy.

As for visiting them the following year, I would have to think about that. I was keen to go to the States with Ted, and I didn't know if I'd be able to afford two trips, in terms of both time and money. But I decided to write back to Jimmy at once, a nice letter, and I began to think about what I could send the kids for Christmas. Suddenly I remembered how depressed I'd felt when I saw the letter sitting in the post-box, and to think of it now, I felt ashamed.

10

From early November onwards, Franca and Davide were engaged in a yearly exercise which frayed both their nerves and mine. Even up in my apartment I could hear them shouting and bickering about it. In the commercial equivalent of pouring a gallon into a pint pot, they stocked their shop for Christmas, while retaining a full supply of everyday products. Franca masterminded where the things would go, and bossed Davide around even more than usual.

Such mundane things as tinned tomatoes and bottled passata, flour, pasta and sugar would be arranged in precarious heaps in odd corners of the shop, and the shelves left free would be crammed with chocolates, *pannetone* cakes in the shape of stars and bells; and huge bars of nougat. Franca herself put together gift baskets, with packets of dried wild mushrooms, bottles of olive oil infused with truffle, expensive sweets; all liberally padded beneath with shredded crêpe paper, and embellished on top with star-spangled cellophane, and glossy ribbons. There was a degree of ostentation which in the end didn't really amount to much. The pictures on the cake-boxes did more than justice to the modest, light fruit-cakes within. The image promised more than that, promised happiness, promised Christmas itself for a few thousand lire. Behind all the extravagance was a marked sense of unease. In the past, the local people had had so little that now they were anxious to flaunt their wealth, to prove to themselves as well as to others that their riches were real, and that they could afford luxurious fripperies far beyond the wildest dreams of their grandparents. That there was more show than substance to many of the things did not bother them a whit, but I had been disappointed the preceding Christmas, when I was given a magnificent blue and gold tin of chocolates, only to find that it was craftily lined in such a way that it was only half full, and there was nothing like as many chocolates as I had hoped or imagined there would be.

Fabiola gave me a huge hamper for Christmas. It wasn't one of Franca's confections, it was from a smart café in Perugia. I was embarrassed by the size and splendour of it, and I didn't feel comfortable taking such a gift from her when I didn't really like her much. When she called to deliver the hamper, she asked what I would be doing for Christmas. I told her that I would be in S. Giorgio, and then I was going to Venice for a few days at New Year. I asked her what she had planned.

'We'll be together for a family Christmas here, and then Pietro and I are going to the Seychelles for ten days.' She twiddled at the heavy jewellery on her fingers, but didn't seem particularly enthusiastic about the thought of the holidays.

I told Franca about this later that day, when she called up to see me. She was impressed with the gift, and very amused by the news about the holiday. 'She must have caught up with him at last then. The whole of S. Giorgio knows that Pietro's been sleeping with Silvia – you know that woman who owns the perfume shop in Via Cavour? Except for you, Fabiola must be the only person who didn't know about it.' Franca was always highly amused by my shortcomings as a gossip, at my slowness to pick up on the crises and scandals that were happening all around me, and my lack of slick delight when I did find out. Even though I didn't much care for Fabiola, I wasn't amused to hear that Pietro had cheated on her, and that most of the village was laughing at her.

'I suppose he'll be trying to make it up to her all over Christmas,' Franca speculated. 'She'll do well. Imagine going to the Seychelles for New Year. Still, if she'd been smart, she could have done even better for herself. Do you know Pietro's brother Riccardo?' I did. He was also in business in the area, and often called into the factory where I worked. I had done odd bits of translating for him. He was as stupid as he was rich, and he was very rich.

'A few years ago,' Franca said, 'his wife Marisa found out that he was having an affair with his secretary. She made such a scene – packed up and went back to her mother's house, taking their little girl with her. Riccardo worships that child. He couldn't believe what was happening. She told him she'd divorce him, and then wouldn't let him see her or the child, or speak to either of them, not even by phone, for over a week. He was distracted. I'll tell you, she really made him crawl. He bought her a mink jacket, promised to take her to Paris, gave her a diamond brooch worth a mint. She eventually agreed to go back to him, but told him that if it happened again, that was it. The funny part was, she'd been having an affair with someone else while he was busy with the secretary, and she only blew the whistle on him out of spite, because her lover had ditched her and gone back to his own wife. I know that she's had at least one other lover since then, but Riccardo's such an idiot that he never found out. And after the last time, he got such a fright about the possibility of losing his daughter that now he hardly dares look at another woman, much less get into bed with one.' There were few things Franca enjoyed more than such a tale as this.

'Fat chance of something like that happening to me,' she added, more in regret, seemingly, than in pride. 'Who'd run off with Davide, with his pot-belly and his bald head and his nonsense? And even if they did, and he wanted to make up for it afterwards, where would all the money for the treats come from, eh? Who breaks their back six days a week selling pasta and cheese, anyway? Who has all the good ideas about how to run the shop better? I'd like to see Davide try to make it up to me for cheating on me by buying me a present with the money I'd earned in the first place!'

Every year Fabiola and Pietro had a Christmas party at their house, and every year I was invited. I didn't want to go, but I felt that this time I had to: I hadn't been there the preceding year, and also I felt a sort of obligation, because of my working for Pietro. There was pragmatism in it too. I knew that there would be local business people there, and that perhaps a bit of freelance translating might come from it, and so I went along.

The first problem was trying to find a suitable gift for Fabiola. That was always a difficulty and a source of resentment to me. I couldn't afford to give her an expensive present, and Fabiola wasn't interested in anything but the best. The idea that it was the thought that counted would have struck her as a very odd notion. The first year I was in S. Giorgio, when I didn't know her very well and I had very little money, I gave her a standard-sized *pannettone* for Christmas. In the shop where I bought it, they stuck a big red bow on the box for me, and I thought it looked like a reasonable thing to give someone – well, I'd have been quite contented if someone had given it to me. When I went to Fabiola's house, I gave her the cake as soon as I went through the door. She didn't actually utter the words 'Thank you,' but whipped the box out of sight, gave a little smile, and led me into the drawing room. She made no reference to it, but there was no failing to notice the massive *pannettone*, at least four times the size of the one I had brought, sitting on a small table. It looked like a house altar dedicated to some male fertility god.

There was such a difference between Fabiola and Franca in this regard. Franca still got a childish thrill even out of the smallest and most simple gift. Her imagination was still alive, while Fabiola's had been dulled by wealth. I remember when we were growing up in Ireland, how much I used to look forward to all the special food – not just the turkey and the pudding, but the boxes of chocolates and even the fruit my father would buy for us on Christmas Eve: the grapes, and the big soft wet pears. I never wanted to lose my sense of occasion. I had a bottle of Calvados I was hoarding until Ted arrived for Christmas. I used to take it out of the cupboard and look at it, and then put it away again. It was salutary to look at people like Fabiola, Pietro and their friends, because it was as if they had rubbed the magic lantern, and been given all the riches they wished for, but they were afraid to admit, sitting in the middle of this plenty, that it had failed to make them happy.

I did feel very sorry for Fabiola the night of the party. As soon as she opened the door to me, I could see how nervous she was. She was more heavily made up than usual, and was wearing a short skirt of black quilted satin, together with a sort of spangly blouse. I remembered the bit of gossip Franca had told me, and I realized why Fabiola looked so fraught. She must have been aware that the situation between herself and Pietro was by now a topic of speculation and gossip all over town. Fabiola's happiness came not from her wealth and beauty, but from the admiration and envy her wealth and beauty evoked in other people. In the same way, she wasn't unhappy now because Pietro had gone off with another woman, but because she knew that people were talking and laughing about it. There was no one she could trust, not even these 'friends' whom she had invited to her home, and who now arrived with gifts of champagne, and were so sweetly greeted, so fondly kissed, and so deeply feared.

Pietro took my coat in the hall. He also looked tense and miserable, as he had done all week at work. Fabiola kept calling him 'Darling' – 'Give Aisling a drink, Darling,' 'Darling, will you introduce Aisling to everybody.' At the start of the evening it sounded merely phoney to me, but by the end of the night her tone had changed, to one of deep sarcasm.

It wasn't a very big party – five couples and me. The only guest I recognized was Pietro's brother Riccardo, who introduced me to his wife, Marisa. She looked me over from head to toe with one brief, cold glance, and she obviously didn't think much of what she saw. They were sitting beside a couple who told me they lived in Bologna. Pietro said that I was from Ireland, and the usual question followed: Is there still fighting in Ireland? I said that there was, but not as much as in Sicily and Calabria. I also explained that the violence was only in a small part of Ireland, and not in the area where I came from.

'And can you tell me please,' said the man from Bologna, 'who is fighting in Ireland? Is it English fighting Irish or Catholics fighting Protestants?'

People always ask me this and I hate it when they do, because there's no simple answer, and they're not interested in a complicated one, in fact they're usually not interested in the answer at all. I could see how pleased the man was that he had been able to ask such an informed and incisive question. He didn't really care who was killing whom or why. People ask you about Ireland who you know would be hard pressed to pick it out on a map, who could easily confuse it with Spitzbergen. Not long after I came to Italy Franca remarked to me one day, 'I suppose you're a very good skier.' I couldn't for the life of me understand what put that idea in her head. I must admit that there have been times when I've been asked about the situation in Ireland and just to avoid the long tedious explanations that might follow I've spiked their conversational guns by opening my eyes wide and saying, 'Fighting? In Ireland? Why not at all, there's no trouble in Ireland.' I knew anyway that for the rest of the night they would forget about Ireland and my being from it, and would ask me, 'And do you have this sort of food in England?' 'And do you have this particular custom in England at Christmas?'

Over dinner, everybody was keen to try out their old broken fragments of school English, asking me if what they said was correct, asking me for the English words for all the things on the table: the cloth, the knives, the plates. Fabiola, who prided herself on her inability to cook, had brought in the caterers. Usually meals in the house were made by a housekeeper, who came every day to cook and bake and clean, while Fabiola was still asleep in bed, or out shopping, or down in the factory, sitting in Pietro's office complaining to him. Before I left the house, Franca had said, 'You'll either get oysters or *bruschetta*,' that is, either a very sophisticated menu, or simple peasant fare. Fabiola had opted for the latter, which had become very fashionable. The grander the dinner, the more likely you were to find *polenta* and sausage on your fine bone-china plate. All Fabiola's guests rose to the occasion, and cooed with delight, as though they were sated with caviare, and it was a rare treat for them to eat such ordinary food.

Fabiola didn't eat anything at all. She served herself tiny portions and then pushed them around her plate with a fork. She had once told me about being at a dinner, and at the end of the night, one of the men in the group had said to her, 'How do you do it, Fabiola? At the end of an evening when everyone else looks tired, you look just as stunningly beautiful as you did when you arrived.' 'And I'll tell you what the secret is, Aisling,' she had said to me proudly. 'When I go out to dinner, I never, ever eat. It ruins your make-up, especially your lipstick. I pretend to, of course, but I never eat a single thing.'

'Maybe I shouldn't ask this while we're eating,' Riccardo said, 'but did anyone see the programme on television the other night about people who eat insects?'

'Oh yes,' said the woman from Bologna delightedly. 'Wasn't it horrible!'

'It was all about these people, I don't remember where, Africa or Australia or somewhere, and they eat insects. All sorts, even grubs and things like that, I could hardly believe it.' Marisa stared at her husband with contempt. She was the only one who took no part in the ensuing animated conversation. Maybe it's because I'm not married and have no desire ever to be so that I have a morbid fascination with married couples. I look at them and I wonder what brought them together, what keeps them together. I suppose it's a bit like the way people who've never had any contact with Catholicism look at nuns and wonder how they live the life they do. One thing I always notice with married people is how much they need other married couples to bolster them up, to reinforce their way of life. They seem to depend on that, and to see people who aren't married as a sort of a threat, so they pretend to pity them. The man from Bologna was talking about his wife as if she weren't there. The topic of conversation had moved on to children.

'My wife wants a baby,' he said loudly. 'I keep telling her it's too much trouble. We were able to come here tonight, and we'll be going ski-ing early in the New Year. Do you think we could do all that if we had a baby? Children are far too much trouble, they take up too much of your time and energy. Still, never let it be said that I've denied my wife anything. We've been trying for a year now, seems like maybe she can't have them. I think it's just as well, but I suppose we'll keep trying for a while longer.' He didn't seem to see that his wife was folding and unfolding her napkin in an obsessive way, nor that her head was bent lower and lower as he went on talking. What I found even more surprising was that no one else seemed to think that there was anything unusual in what the man said. His wife suddenly lifted her head, and looked at him with pure hatred. No one noticed that either.

'I think you're quite right,' said another woman. 'It spoils your figure when you have children, and you wouldn't believe how much time they take up, and how they change things in your life. Do you know, I have a friend who has three children. Three little children! How they manage I simply don't know.'

I was struck that night by the sheer indestructibility of the bourgeois. For a moment I saw the whole scene as it would have been a hundred years ago, saw us all sitting there in frock-coats and long stiff dresses, and it didn't seem at all incongruous – myself there as the foreigner, the governess, the poor relation; the same snobbery, the same ugly, expensive possessions and stupid fashions, the same seeming manners thinly masking vulgarity and mental crudeness. I thought it was extraordinary how easily it could have been the distant past. It was as if down here in the provinces they didn't know that there had been two world wars, that things were different now. They were like a lost tribe, and I felt that they would have been devastated if they moved beyond the little confines of their world, would have found it impossible to cope if they had not been bolstered up by each other, and by their money.

It was a joyless evening. Fabiola was palpably unhappy. When the meal was over and we had moved away from the table, she came over and sat down beside me. I said the dinner had been very good, and she smiled briefly and shrugged. She asked me again what I was doing for Christmas and New Year, and as I told her, I could see that she wasn't listening. Her eyes wandered uneasily over the room, as if she couldn't understand what all these people were doing in her house, or who they were. The couple from Bologna had ended up sitting beside each other on a yellow sofa. He was dragging on a cigarette, and they barely spoke to each other. When she did say anything, he lifted his head impatiently, and answered her shortly.

When I came home from the party, I went into the bathroom, and I saw someone there I didn't recognize. Then I realized that it was me, reflected in the mirror. I went back into the sitting room and kicked off my shoes. Then I started to cry, because it had been such a miserable evening that to come home from it and weep seemed inevitable. I was quite certain that at that very moment the woman from Bologna was also in tears, and that Fabiola was standing in her fitted kitchen, surrounded by the wreckage of dinner and bawling like a child. To know this was little consolation to me. I had compromised myself by going there. I had pretended to like those people and to be nice to them for my own ends, when I really had nothing but contempt for them. What had I expected? It served me right that I was crying now.

I went to bed hoping that I would feel better the next morning, but I slept badly, dreamt wildly, and woke up feeling worse than I had done in a long time. I went to Adolfo's for breakfast, but that didn't help me either, for once, it made it worse. There was a woman in front of me with a little boy. He was about three years old, and he wanted a sandwich.

'Tomato and cheese? What about one with tomato and cheese?' said the child's mother, while Adolfo rummaged through the pile of sandwiches with a pair of tongs to find a suitable one. Having done so, he offered it to the child, but the little boy jerked his head away, and did not take the sandwich. He wailed loudly and horribly, and then hit the glass front of the counter with the flat of his hand. 'I don't think he wants tomato and cheese,' said Adolfo, calmly replacing the sandwich. 'What about ham and cheese, then?' said the mother to the little boy, and Adolfo started to rummage again. I felt my temper move slowly towards boiling point. It was all I could do not to grab the little boy and shake him till his teeth rattled, all I could do not to scream to the mother, 'He's only three, for Christ's sake! There are kids starving in the world, give him any sort of God-forsaken sandwich, and let him learn to be grateful for what he has. If he's as spoiled as this now, what'll he be like when he grows up?'

And then I thought: He'll probably be like Adolfo, whose second sandwich had been accepted, Adolfo who was smiling beatifically and reaching up to get a fancy chocolate out of a jar to give to the little boy. He wouldn't be like me, now sullenly mumbling my order for coffee and cake. While I was drinking my *cappuccino*, I remembered what my grandmother always used to say: 'Other people's children are easy reared.' I could never make up my mind. I hated the way I had been brought up, and I knew it had done me terrible harm. Yet when I saw the Italian children being spoiled and cosseted, I used to think instinctively that they needed a taste of stronger medicine, that a clip on the ear would do them a power of good. Then I would remember what that had done to me, and I'd be confused. I suppose the best course was somewhere between the two, and I was glad that I didn't have kids, and didn't have to try to find that right balance.

I had tried to send particularly appealing presents to Jimmy's kids that year. Usually I just sent them sweets, but this time I had wanted to give them something more. I had been amazed at how difficult this had turned out to be. At first I thought I would send them something to wear, and then I realized that I didn't know their sizes, and I didn't want to risk sending things that wouldn't fit. I also remembered that I had hated getting clothes as a present when I was small. When I was Sinead's age, I had wanted a child-sized umbrella, but of course that didn't mean that she would want one, and in any case, it would be too awkward a shape to wrap and post. I ended up sending Michael a teddy bear, and Sinead a doll with a china face. It had taken me a whole evening to wrap and pack the doll in such a way that I felt sure it would arrive in Dublin still in one piece. The toys cost me a bomb, but it was my last resort. I had no other ideas, and if I waited any longer, they would never arrive in time for Christmas.

Christmas is about the only festival I don't like. Sometimes I even think that you're not supposed to like it, that it's been deliberately planned to be as difficult as possible. It falls at the end of the year, in the middle of winter, when your resistance is low, and your defences are weak. Then there's all that stuff about family and children. Well, I don't have any family or any kids, and I'm not a child myself any more. But Christmas acts like an emotional cattle-prod on me, and makes me aware of how alone in the world I am. That's something I can ignore or cope with or even enjoy at other times of the year. My parents are dead, Jimmy and I will never be close again. For some reason, it can upset me at Christmas to realize that. But I always fight against easy nostalgia, because it's a pack of lies. Eventually everything has to become the past, because life goes on, as it must. You can't hold on to the past, and if you try to do that, especially if you try to hold on to your childhood, you find that it goes anyway. And the punishment is that you don't have any life as an adult and you find out too late that you can't hold on to your childhood either, and so you're left with nothing. I've seen that happen to people and, whatever else, I've fought to make sure it doesn't happen to me.

Fabiola's party had been six days before Christmas, and Ted was to come down from Florence on Christmas Eve. I thought that the days until his arrival would never pass. After the party, I felt as if I had lost a layer of my skin, and that I had no defences left against anything. There was a strange atmosphere that year because of all the things that had happened in Eastern Europe in the preceding months. I hated reading those gloating articles in the papers about the happy shoppers from East Berlin going home through the Wall at dusk with all their brightly coloured packages. Then when I read about the revolution in Romania and about the young people in Timisoara being shot, I cried, and it didn't help to know that I was really crying for myself.

We watched the news reports on television in Franca's apartment on Christmas Eve night. She had invited us up to eat salt cod with her family, and she was unashamedly curious about Ted. Although in the past she had always poured scorn on America and Americans, I could see that in his case she was prepared to make an exception. Ted was one of those nice guys everybody likes. Davide's mother and Lucia and the whole family took to him. Every time his back was turned, Franca grinned and winked at me with delight. She had been working hard in the shop right up until dinner time, and she was tired. They had done a good pre-Christmas trade, she told me, and now she was determined to do nothing but enjoy herself for a couple of days.

Christmas Day was sunny and mild in S. Giorgio. I remember the olive groves on the slopes below the walls of the town, and how from a distance they looked a sort of smoky purple colour. I remember the light on the façade of the church, and all the crowds of people milling around, dressed in new clothes. In Romania, they shot the Ceausescus. We heard later that they showed the bodies on Romanian television many times that day, and played Beethoven's 'Ode to Joy' over the pictures. I rang Jimmy. When the kids came on the line to thank me for the presents they both sounded shy. I could hear Nuala prompting little Michael in whispers. They probably didn't know what to make of me. I suppose it was easier for them to believe in Santa than in this faraway Aunt they never saw, who was just a fancy present and a voice coming out of a telephone.

In the coming weeks, we were to read about the Ceausescus' Christmas presents, found wrapped in spangly paper under a Christmas tree. There were cards on the mantelpiece 'to darling Mummy and Daddy'. They'd tried to make the whole country think of them as Mummy and Daddy; many of the secret police turned out to be orphans who'd been chosen for that very reason. They'd been taught to be loyal to the Ceausescus not in the way you're loyal to a national leader, but as you're loyal to parents.

I cooked a chicken for dinner. I asked Ted did he want to ring his parents, and he said no, that they wouldn't be expecting to hear from him, that if he rang they might even think that something was wrong. That night we opened the bottle of Calvados I'd been saving up, and I drank far too much of it.

11

'When I was a child, I couldn't understand how telegraph poles worked. I thought all the words went down the wires, and if you cut a wire, language would drip out of it like water from a broken pipe.' Ted laughed. We were on a train somewhere north of Bologna, and the flat land was foggy, as it usually is there for most of the winter. The telegraph poles fled past the windows. We were on our way to Venice for the New Year. I was glad to be away from S. Giorgio for a while, glad to be on a train. Sometimes I like being in public, anonymous places, because it's easier to talk there. Later, if I came to regret what I said, or if something bad happened, I wouldn't be reminded of it every time I looked at a certain corner of my own room. There was only one other person in the compartment with us, a middle-aged woman who was sitting opposite me. She was asleep.

Ted and I started to talk then on the train about things we had thought when we were children, things we hadn't understood, words that we had been confused about. Then we began to talk about dreams, the sort of dreams we had had when we were children, and then the dreams we had now. I always think you have to know someone really well before you can tell them about your dreams – well, given the way I dream, it's best not to buttonhole total strangers with them, or they'd run a mile. I tried Ted with one of my least-worst nightmares, and he said 'Wow,' then I risked a more graphic one. I told him about the dream of the maggots eating my head, and this time he didn't say anything. I looked out of the window. We were still fog-bound.

I carefully worked my way around to what I had wanted to talk about when I introduced the whole question of dreams, and asked Ted did he ever have waking dreams. He looked at me carefully, and asked me what I meant. Before I could reply, we heard a ringing sound – a food trolley was coming up the corridor. The woman sitting opposite me woke up, and bought herself a coffee and a ham roll. The smell of coffee filled the compartment. Ted and I went on whispering to each other in English.

I told him I meant when you get an image fixed in your head – an image, rather than an idea, and it's not the image of something you've seen, but it's as powerful as a dream, and you can't get it out of your mind. He said no, that never happened to him. Sometimes he got thoughts stuck in his head, memories of things he'd seen or done, particularly things he didn't like, and felt bad about. He might feel guilty, but he knew it was too late to do anything. He asked me what sort of thing I meant, and I told him about the hanged woman, who had come into my mind at least three times since the night of Fabiola's party. I told him it wasn't me that was being hanged, and I didn't feel suicidal when I had this image in my mind. I felt troubled, but not so much on my own account. It worried me because it seemed such an unhealthy thing to think about, and I told him that I did try not to dwell on it. The woman opposite me had finished her coffee and roll. She took out a little tin box full of tiny liquorice sweets, and offered them to us. We each took one, smiled and thanked her.

Ted asked me if I had told anybody else about this, apart from him. I said that I hadn't. He asked me, didn't I think I ought to? I said I probably should, but I had been to doctors before, and they didn't seem to be able to help, especially here in Italy, that I felt too different. He asked me, aren't you worried about this, and I said, well, I supposed I was. The woman appeared to have fallen asleep again. I'm always struck by how vulnerable and innocent people look when they're sleeping. I told Ted not to worry, and he looked angry and whispered, 'Jesus, Aisling, how can I not worry?' I looked out at the fog again. It's amazing how, if you never tell anybody anything, you can convince yourself that the weirdest things are normal, or that they're at least a lot less bizarre than you would consider them if they were happening to someone else. I had embarked gingerly on this conversation, as if I had half thought he might accept it as normal, and not pass much comment. Maybe I had thought he might reciprocate with some strange and violent mental movies of his own. But now I knew that that couldn't have happened, for if he had ever given any indication, however slight, of being violent or disturbed, I would never have taken up with him, I would have been too frightened. Then I could see that perhaps he was frightened too. Certainly, he was worried. I stroked his hand to reassure him, but I don't think it made much difference.

We were to stay in the apartment of an old friend of Ted's who lived in Venice. He told me her name was Maria. He had suggested to her that they exchange apartments for a few days, so that she could stay in Florence. She had already made other plans, and was going to New York, but said that her apartment would be empty, and if we wanted to borrow it, we were welcome. She was to leave for Milan shortly after we arrived, and would fly to the States the following morning.

The train arrived in Venice on time. I always like going to Venice, I like it when you go out of the railway station and there's a canal where there should be a road. I know it's corny, but I do like it. I can understand why millions of people visit Venice every year, and why they think it's the most beautiful city in the world.

We went by *vaporetto* first to St Mark's Square, and then we made our way by foot through the narrow streets and over the tiny bridges until we got to the right place. Ted rang the bell, and a voice spoke through the grille by the door. '*Chi c'è?*' Ted said his name, and the door buzzed and clicked open, we went up a flight of wooden stairs, where a woman was waiting by an open door.

I disliked Maria as soon as I saw her, and I felt sure that she didn't like me. One day, when I was complaining to Ted about one of the other women in the factory where I worked, he had remarked that it was strange how I got on much better with men than with women. I immediately denied this, but later when I thought about it, I was forced to admit that he was right. I got on much better with Pietro than with Fabiola, and I still didn't feel at ease with my sister-in-law Nuala, not even on the phone. With men I rarely felt that instant animosity on first meeting which I so often felt with women, and which I now experienced towards Maria.

She wasn't at all what I had expected. I had asked Ted if she was American, and he had said, 'No, she's from Scotland.' If he hadn't told me, I would never have guessed it. She spoke in a neutral accent, in which I could distinguish no apparent regional differentiation or inflection, apart from the odd mid-Atlantic word or phrase, which puzzled me even more. Like me, she had taken on the protective shell of Italian elegance, but she had done it more successfully because she had more money. From a glance at her clothes, her opulent apartment and the pile of Mandarina Duck luggage at the door I could easily tell that she wasn't dependent on factory discounts. But what disconcerted me most of all was that Ted had called her a 'friend', and as soon as I saw them together I knew there had been more to it than that. Even I could see that the jealousy I felt at this was irrational. While it was clear that they had been lovers it was also clear that it was over now, and the relationship had tapered off into friendship. It bothered me because it was a situation I couldn't understand. I tried to imagine myself five years later, lending the apartment in S. Giorgio to Ted and some other woman for a week, making coffee for them before I left, as Maria did now. I knew that I could never do that, and it was beyond me how she could do it.

When we went into the kitchen, I walked straight over to the window, which overlooked a narrow canal. 'It must be beautiful to live here,' I said, more from nerves than sincerity.

'Beautiful? Here? Are you serious?' Maria said, banging the coffee pot against the side of the bin to knock out the damp grounds. 'Living in Venice is hell. It's like living in a theme park. If you just come here for a visit it's hard to get a sense of how unreal it is, even what a strange place it is. There's no real community here, you do realize that, don't you? All the real Venetians moved out years ago. There's nobody left but a bunch of old money-mad contessas, asking outrageous rents for a few damp rooms in some crumbling old dump of a palazzo. They don't give a damn about culture, they don't even give a damn about Venice. All they want is to make as much money as possible, and to have their picture taken with Jack Nicholson during the film festival. And then there are the tourists. Sometimes I don't blame the Venetians for ripping them off, they really do ask for it. The vulgarity of it can get you down, the endless swarms with their video cameras and their gondolier's straw hats, pestering you to know how to get to St Mark's Square every time you step outside.'

'Yeah,' Ted said. He was putting out cups and sugar, and he knew obviously where everything was kept in the kitchen. 'Bigger cities like Rome, or even Florence, manage to absorb the tourists they attract. The areas tourists go to in any city are always really limited anyway. The majority just stick with the main sights, so there are always quiet areas, if you just know where to look for them.'

'You've come at a good time, though,' said Maria. 'It's usually quite quiet around the end of the year, although of course the weather can be bad.' She poured out the coffee and while we were drinking it, she started to interrogate me. That's the only way I can describe it, and it wasn't the first time it had happened to me either. When I was growing up I had always been taught that it was rude to ask too many questions about people, but I had started to notice that lots of people now felt free to cross-question others, and to consider that the process passed for conversation. Where did I live? What was my job? How long had I been living in S. Giorgio? How long had I been in Italy? Where had I lived before that? Had I liked living in Paris? Why then had I left it? I gave her vague, abrupt answers, my tone becoming colder and more openly impatient with each one. The problem is, that when people are crass enough to grill you like this they either don't notice or don't care how infuriating you find it. Far from backing off, Maria was even a bit nettled by some of my sullen responses, and became even more persistent. For instance, when she asked me why I moved to Italy, I shrugged and said, 'I just did it.'

'Oh, come on,' she said, 'people don't just move about like that.'

'Well, I do.'

'Did you have to leave Ireland?'

'Of course not. I chose to.'

Suddenly she became quite hostile. 'I can't understand the way some people choose to live nowadays, really I can't, wandering about all over the place the way they do. Years ago people had the right idea. They were born in a place and they stayed in it. They had their kids there and they died there. If they wanted to go on holidays they went to the nearest bit of seaside, and if you ask me, they were all a lot happier then. I get sick of people haring around all over the place. You see them here, all these crazy, mixed-up people, misfits in their own countries, people who basically have something wrong with them' (she was staring hard at me as she said this). 'And so they leave their ordinary little town, as if by going to some equally ordinary little town thousands of miles away they'll solve something. The nonsense you come across! I see people here in Venice, maybe the husband Italian and the wife American, and they have kids who are bilingual. Then they're sending them to classes to learn, I don't know, German or French, and they're taking them all over the place for holidays, to see grandparents on the other side of the world. Children only need one language, and to grow up in one place. If they feel rooted and happy there, then they'll stay there and be happy. I don't think I've ever met a bilingual person who couldn't be described as inarticulate in two languages.'

To my amazement, Ted laughed. 'Hey, Maria, lay off that stuff, will you? Still on the same old story. People like me and Aisling, we know what we're about. You're just spoiled, that's all. You sure you want to go to New York for New Year's? Sure you wouldn't like to go to somewhere like Poggibonsi instead?' He was smiling as he said this, and she smiled too. She let him defuse the situation because she was still fond of him, and because she was still fond of him, I reasoned, she was jealous of me. She looked at her watch, and ground out the cigarette she'd been smoking. 'I'd better go, if I'm not to miss the train.' Ted wanted to help her take her bags to the station, but she insisted that she could manage on her own. She gave us a few brief instructions about light switches and watering plants before she left. When we were saying goodbye to her, I was able to wish her the best, because I knew that a few hours later I'd be in her bed with Ted, and I knew that she knew. So I thanked her for the loan of the apartment and I gave her a great big smile, and suddenly she looked lonely and vulnerable. I felt very small minded, which I know I often am. I was glad when she had gone.

We listened to her descending the stairs, and then Ted said, 'Poor Maria. Take no notice of her; she's a sweet person, but she has this hang-up about belonging somewhere.' He told me then that her Scottishness was a fairly tenuous thing. Her parents were both from Edinburgh. Her father had been a business man whose work took him all over the world, and the family had always gone with him. Maria had told Ted that she knew it had had a disastrous effect on her. She was born in Kuala Lumpur, and until the age of twenty, she had never lived longer than two years in any one country. She learned to walk in Sydney, started school in Tokyo, and during her childhood lived in Stockholm, Paris, Hong Kong and Manila, amongst other places. Her parents decided not to send her to boarding school in Britain, so she attended international schools where they existed, and local schools where they didn't. 'The first time she told me about it,' Ted said, 'I thought it sounded great, but she said, "Well, it wasn't great. It was hell." She went to university when she was eighteen. Her parents had always told her that she was from Scotland, so as soon as she had freedom of choice, she headed straight for the place she had been taught to think of as home. Perhaps it's not surprising that she hated it. She didn't *feel* that she belonged there,' Ted said, 'and that was always a big thing with her, this need to feel at home. I used to always tell her what a drag home can be, but she never believed me. She had been convinced that she would feel she belonged in Scotland, and she was stunned when she didn't. The other students didn't regard her as Scottish, and no wonder. She'd hardly ever been there until she started college. At the end of her first year she dropped out, transferred to Paris, and did her degree there. She told me that she didn't "belong" in Paris either, but she never expected to, so it was no big deal. It was just like the rest of her life had been up until then. But she's never lost that idea that there're some places and some ways of living that other people can tap into but which are closed to her, and that if only she could find a place where she felt at home, she'd be happy.

'She holds it against her family that they gave her the sort of life they did. I think she particularly resents that after her father retired, her parents went back to Edinburgh and bought a house there. They're happy and settled there now, and somehow that makes it even worse for her. As for her job, I don't know if that's been a help or a hindrance. She works for a big international auction house, and she travels all over the place, mainly in the States and Europe, looking at furniture for them. It's a really good job; the sort of job a lot of people would kill for, but she doesn't love it. You can see what a great place she has here: she owns all this antique furniture, and those paintings – and she earns a lot of money, but she's the most unrooted, maybe even the most unhappy person I've ever known. She would deny this, I know, but I always think Maria believes that somewhere there is a place where she could be contented – if only she could find it. She believes that there are places where you can find happiness, just as there are places where you can find wild mushrooms.' I felt even meaner and more small minded than I had done earlier.

We stayed in Venice for four days. At first the weather wasn't good, and then on the second day the fog lifted, and we went out across the lagoon to the islands. I remember the coloured houses of Burano, and the Byzantine church on Torcello. I always think that it's impossible to predict the impression particular places will make on you. Often, especially in Italy, I found that the big famous monuments left me cold, but that some small detail of them would be unforgettable, like a mosaic of Noah's ark high up in St Mark's. I remember that, and I remember the long, dark stern-faced Madonna on a gold field in Torcello, and the Last Judgement on the back wall of the church, where black devils forked the damned into the flames. Two days later, we visited the Jewish quarter, where the buildings are taller than in other parts of Venice, to accommodate all the people who were forced to live there at the time when it was the only part of Venice where

Jews were allowed to live. Now it was almost deserted. We visited an empty synagogue, and looked in the tiny bright window of a kosher grocery shop. There was a memorial to all those who had been taken from the ghetto and died in concentration camps all over Europe. Sometimes, standing on railway platforms in Italy, a goods train would go through at high speed, and I would shudder when I thought of what had happened in Europe not so long ago. The paintings in the church seemed a quaint fancy in comparison to the reality that had emptied the ghetto.

The fog came back on New Year's Eve, and made all the lights of the city pearly, including the little coloured lights on the Christmas tree in St Mark's Square. The city was rife with cats, their eyes full of cold appetite, like sharks, intent on their own concerns, and closed in their own worlds. We had dinner in a restaurant that night, and there was an air of excitement in the city as the year ran down to its conclusion. For days now people had been throwing firecrackers around. In S. Giorgio they had been tossing them in front of unsuspecting people since well before Christmas. Now in Venice the noise was building up. The steady monotonous banging noise made it sound as though the city were being shelled. Ted asked me at dinner, 'What will it be like in S. Giorgio tonight?' and I laughed.

'It'll be like the end of the world,' I said. 'At midnight, there'll be the most almighty explosion of firecrackers and fireworks, as if it were the most important night ever, as if everyone's lives and fortunes were going to change in the morning. The whole sky will be lit up, and it'll be like it's to mark something new, something wonderful. And then tomorrow morning the silent pall of provinciality will fall over the place again, and people's lives will go on exactly the same as they always did, and will for ever.'

12

One morning in January, a little convoy left S. Giorgio for the mountains. Franca packed her mother-in-law and Davide into the car, together with four bottles of *spumante* and some cakes and chocolates she had taken from the shop, including a four-kilo cake, wrapped in gold foil and tied with a red ribbon, that looked like a gift-wrapped bomb. Lucia and Ted came in my car, and shortly after a quarter to eight, we all set off.

Almost as soon as we left the village, by the high back road, instead of the route I usually took to the lower village and the plain, we were into territory where tourists rarely ventured. It was a strange phenomenon, for every year thousands of people visited S. Giorgio, but invariably went back down the hill afterwards, as if there were a line on the road at the back of the town, beyond which they were forbidden to go. The real reason that they didn't go there was because the guidebooks didn't tell them to. Perhaps in any case they wouldn't have liked the scenery, for there was a harshness up in the mountains which there was not in the softer, lower hills, with their olives and vines and ploughed fields, with the gentle open contours of the land. Here, the valleys were high and closed, the roads steep and twisted. We passed outcrops of friable white rock, from which grew stunted trees and bushes. Sometimes the land had fallen away, and the whole root system of the tree could be seen. For all its harshness, I thought it had a real beauty of its own, unlike the soft, easy loveliness of the lower land, with its muted colours. Not least of the mountain's attractions was the view it afforded. Looking back, we could see S. Giorgio now far below us. From that angle you couldn't see the new town, just the back of the village, neatly walled, and pale in the clear light of the morning. It looked as it must have done so long ago, at the time when town planning was an innate skill, when people still lived on a human scale, and did not build sprawling, malfunctioning towns. There was a light mist on the floor of the valley, so we could see only faintly the sprawling glitter of the towns down on the plain, but off in the distance was clearly visible the chain of blue mountains that stretched away to the south.

I had been up here many times before, but it was Ted's first visit, and he was enthusiastic, much to Lucia's amusement, who thought it the dullest place in the world, and couldn't imagine what anybody could see in it. We drove through a tiny village, completely closed and shuttered up. 'Nobody stirring there today,' Ted said. 'That's because there is nobody there,' Lucia said. 'Very few people live up here now. When Mama was growing up there were lots of villages and isolated farms, but now there's hardly anybody. They got smart,' she laughed, 'and moved down the hill, the way Mama did when she got married.' I had heard before that the population hadn't grown much for twenty years, but had simply relocated, with people moving down the hill to work in shops and factories and offices. Now the hills were empty, but for a few remaining farmers, such as Franca's brother, whom we were on our way to visit, and a sprinkling of foreigners, who bought old farmhouses and restored them, grew lavender and kept bees and did not mix with the locals.

'I think this is great,' Ted said. 'I think I'd like to live here. Maybe I'll buy a house and fix it up. What do you say, Lucia? What about that one there – that would be nice, wouldn't it?' She almost fell off her seat laughing. He was pointing at a place that was almost a complete ruin. 'He's crazy, your boyfriend, Aisling.'

I didn't join in the laughter. Lucia had obviously developed a real adolescent crush on Ted, which was normal, if you think about it, as she was an adolescent. I couldn't reason that way at the time, and I was irritated by the way she was flirting and giggling with him, and how he was teasing her. I had looked forward so much to this day out, but already I was aware of a black mood closing in around me. The silent huff I sank into was a waste of energy, for neither Ted nor Lucia took any notice of it, and went on talking.

'You think I'm kidding?' Ted said, trying to keep a straight face. 'I think it would be great. Wouldn't you like to marry a farmer and live up here, have kids, keep hens, stuff like that?'

'You really are crazy,' Lucia said. 'Me? Marry a *contadino*? Nowadays, nobody wants to marry them, don't you know that? They have a marriage bureau in Perugia, and almost all of the men on their books are farmers. Women come up from the south, from Calabria and Sicily and marry them. Nobody here wants them.'

'So it's the bright lights for you then. I suppose you'll be off to Rome as soon as you're eighteen.'

'I didn't say that,' Lucia interjected quickly, suddenly serious. '*Sto bene qui*. I like it here. I like it at home with Mama and Papa. They do that in other countries, go away, but I don't want to do it. When Aisling's not here, I'll get married and move upstairs. If you're happy and you have everything you want in a place, why would you ever go away?'

'Why indeed,' I thought grimly. 'Why bother to live your life when you can let not just your parents, but the whole of society live it for you?'

After a time, the mountains closed in, so that we could no longer see down to the plain. We arrived at the farm almost an hour after we left S. Giorgio. Franca and Davide had arrived just moments before, and were unloading the car. The door of the farmhouse was open, and we all went in. The kitchen was almost empty. Patrizia, Franca's sister-in-law, was making pasta, the wooden board before her already piled with yellow ribbons of tagliatelli. Franca's mother, an old woman in black, was sitting on a low stool beside a blazing wood fire. When we greeted her, she looked as blankly at Davide, her son-in-law, as she did at Ted, a complete stranger. Patrizia was delighted to see everybody again.

'Where are the others?' Franca asked, as Davide carried in the

116

wine and cakes. 'Michele's on the hill, with the second pig,' Patrizia replied. 'The others are down in the barn with the pig that was killed yesterday.'

'We'll go see Michele first.' We went out of the house with Franca, and followed her along a narrow path which wound behind a gentle rise. As we got nearer we could hear a light clink-clink-clink, clear in the air, like a bell being struck. And when we went round the corner and saw what was there, suddenly I felt dizzy, sick to my stomach, and then I felt foolish, for what, after all, had I expected to see on such a visit?

A little huddle of people were standing around a dead pig, which was hanging by its back legs from chains attached to a strong wooden post. The pig had been half split open, and the people gathered around were in the process of cutting it completely in two. The clink-clink noise was the sound of a hammer and chisel against the bones of the pig's spine. The animal's ears were flopped over its eyes, as if it couldn't bear to look at what was happening. The warm open cavity of the body smoked in the cold air. I was glad that we hadn't got there any earlier. The ground was splashed with blood, and a trio of hefty cats sat under an old broken cart a short distance away, impassively waiting to be fed. Michele and the others were delighted to see us, and the pig was ignored for a few moments while a full round of greetings and introductions took place. Michele offered his wrist to be shaken, because his hands were covered with blood. He looked at me very intently, and I felt uncomfortable. Franca slapped the side of the pig admiringly, and it swung lugubriously on its chains. Michele got back to work with his chisel, and Ted took some photos of the pig, which confirmed Lucia's belief that he was crazy.

'The others are down in the barn, you can go and see them if you want,' Michele said, but Grazia, one of the women who had been holding the pig steady, interjected. 'Don't go just yet. Let's see if the wedding has started.' Grazia was huddled up in heavy clothes and boots. Her crude apron was covered in blood. She led us to the edge of the rise, and looking down, in a lower valley far below us, we could see a church with a group of people standing outside. 'I've been watching them all morning,' Grazia said. 'Look, here they are now.' A car pulled up and a figure in white got out.

'It's Paola Calzolari, do you remember her, Franca? She went to live in Frascati and married a man there, but it didn't work out. They had a little daughter, and got divorced three years ago. Now she's living with another man, and she's pregnant again, and this time she wants to do it in church. I suppose she hopes it'll be the last time. Her little girl's to be an attendant. Here she is.'

The figure in white was followed by a child in pink. Some people who had been waiting gathered around them, and they stood for a short while talking. Then they all disappeared into the church, and from where we were, it was as neat and as swift as a clockwork toy. 'Good luck to them, anyway,' Grazia said. She wiped her hands on her apron.

Franca said, 'I always tell Lucia, when the time comes for you to get married, don't settle for a civil service. Go to church, because you're going to need all the help you can get.' They all laughed, and as we turned away, she added, 'Anyway, whatever gets you through your life, grab at it, that's what I always say.'

We turned back to where the pig was hanging. It was so solid, so dead, the cold dead fact of the pig's body hanging there was a shock to me, and it remained in my mind throughout the day.

We left the hill, and the steady clink-clink of metal and bone followed us, as we went down to a shed at the side of the house. When Franca opened the door there was a mixed confusion of voices, noise and light, of greeting and introduction, but above all, the two things that struck me were, first, the coldness of the shed, and second, the stench of blood which had been evident up on the hill, but was much stronger here. I recognized some of the people, and I was introduced to the butcher who had been hired for the day, and was there to oversee the correct preparation of the meat. With a long slender knife he was shaping the fat at the edge of a pig's leg into the familiar shape of a ham, which would then be salted and hung to dry in a cold place. The protruding knob of bone was glossy and white.

Ted and I spent the morning in the shed. After the hams were completed, piles of chops were cut, some set aside for lunch that day, some wrapped for the freezer. Meat was prepared to make salami and sausages. They put a lot of pepper in some of the salami, and then tied a red ribbon to the string around it, so that they could tell it from other salami, the ones that were not *piccante*. For the sausages, the butcher clamped a mincer to the table, and produced a jar of damp grey intestines, which looked like overwashed elastic. A long length of intestine was fitted over the end of the mincer, and by a combination of gently pressing on the meat in the hopper and coaxing along the rapidly filling intestine, a long meaty cord appeared, which the butcher deftly twisted into links. Ted took a turn with the mincer, but he wasn't very good at it, and almost minced his fingers, so he let the butcher take over again.

Around noon, Lucia and I went up to the kitchen, taking with us a pile of sausages and chops to be cooked for lunch. Patrizia and Lucia started to set the table for fifteen people. Franca's mother was still on the little stool, huddled over the fire. She had the saddest face I've ever seen. 'I'm cold,' she said to me. 'I'm always cold. I sit by the fire all day, and no matter what I do, I can never get warm. See,' and she drew her hands away from the blaze and touched my face. She was as cold as marble. It was all I could do not to let her see how repulsed I felt. It was like talking to and being touched by a person who was already dead, and whom the family had simply neglected to bury.

Franca came over and started to poke vigorously at the fire, stoking it up at the back, and raking out the burning embers at the front, where the meat was to be cooked. She opened a wooden chest where the firewood was stored, and took out a huge log. The fire sparked and crackled when she put it on, and flames licked quickly up the side of it. Franca beamed with delight. 'Nothing like a good fire, is there? It's company. I could sit and look at a blaze like that from morning to night. Do you know the old saying, Aisling – "A hearth without a log is like a man without a prick."'

Franca's mother looked confused. 'What's the proper name for it, Franca? I don't remember. The Italian name for the man's thing.'

'Penis.'

'And the woman's thing?'

'Vagina.'

Franca smiled. 'Poor Mama. She only remembers the dialect words for them. They've got a million names in dialect. Probably never needed the Italian words. Not that words matter that much, I suppose.' She lifted a grid-iron down from a hook above the fire, opened it, and began to neatly arrange pork chops on it as she went on talking. 'Things aren't the way they were in Mama's time. They aren't even the way they were in my time, and thank God or whoever for it, that's what I say. All that stuff they told us when I was growing up, to frighten the hell out of us, and it did, too. Sometimes it still puts me off. Sometimes I still feel guilty, even now. Can you believe that? It won't be like that for Lucia. I'd rather she got into the odd scrape, so long as she enjoys herself, so long as she's happy.'

Franca closed the grid-iron, and set it carefully over the raked-out glowing wood embers. Then she took down another grid-iron, and began to prepare the sausages in the same way.

We went on getting ready for lunch – setting out glasses, fetching wine from the cellar, dressing salad, slicing up bread. At about ten to one, Patrizia put the pasta on to cook, and Lucia was sent to call in the workers.

What with the early start, the cold weather and the hard work, everybody was hungry, and more than did justice to the meal, which was a huge affair. One thing that annoyed me was that I didn't get to sit beside Ted. Michele slipped in beside me and throughout the meal kept plying me with more food than I could possibly eat. He also topped up my glass constantly, so that I couldn't keep track of how much I was drinking. I didn't like it that he was so attentive to me, and I kept trying to catch Ted's eye. For a long time he didn't notice me, because he was so busy laughing and eating and talking, and when at last he did look my way he was so delighted with the lunch and life in general that he didn't seem to notice that anything was amiss. I was vexed and angry.

The meal went on and on, as if lunch itself was reluctant to end, trailing off almost two hours later into grace-notes of ice-cream, *spumante*, cheese, chocolates, coffee and liqueurs.

Afterwards, most of the people went back out to work, while Lucia and I helped clear up after the meal. When that was done, Franca called me into the parlour to look at some photographs on the wall. She showed me a picture of her grandmother, her mother's mother, a voluptuous woman with soft eyes. 'Nonna was so big,' Franca said fondly. 'I remember when I was little and she hugged me, I'd almost disappear into her. She had the biggest chest I've ever seen on a woman: each one was like a head.'

When I went back to the shed, Grazia was standing by a bucket which contained the ears and snout of the pig. She lifted them out in turn, and casually scorched the bristles from them with a small blow torch, before throwing them back in the bucket again. Michele was cleaning the table. He poured a glass of white wine over it, which was rubbed well into the grain of the wood before they began to prepare the lard, kneading it and mixing it, and putting it in glass jars to be stored.

By late afternoon, the job was done. All the meat had been butchered, the last links twisted into sausages, all the ribs, the cheeks, the ears: everything had been dealt with. Everyone was satisfied, not least the cats, who had been given the fatty scraps from the lunch. The butcher said that he would be back the following day, to deal with the second pig.

When dusk had fallen, Michele and Patrizia took Ted and me on a tour of the farm. Ted had been in Italy for years, but it was the first time he had been on an Italian farm, and I suspected it was a long time since he had been on a farm anywhere. When Patrizia opened the byre door, and we went in, the warm fug of the animals was strong and comforting after the cold air outside. The six pale cattle who were generating this heat staggered nervously to their feet and stared at us. Back outside again we saw pens full of geese, rabbits, ducks and chickens, and a flock of long-legged Biblical sheep. The sounds and smells of the farm-yard reminded me, not always pleasantly, of growing up on my father's farm in Ireland.

We went into another outhouse, where some of the pork from the day's work was already in store. Apart from the hams and salamis suspended from the beams there were odd-looking pieces of offal, hanging from hooks. I didn't know which bits they were, and I didn't ask. There were buckets full of blood, and the same solid sweet stench which there had been all morning in the shed where the butchering had taken place. Michele reached up to the rafters and lifted down a bunch of grapes which had been hung there months earlier to dry. He offered them to us to taste, and beyond the initial sharpness there was a memory of sweetness locked in the heart of them, as though the sun of the past summer was still contained in these winter grapes.

Then Michele wanted to show us the house too, and so we trooped from one dim, tiny room to another. I felt increasingly nervous. Michele kept standing too close to me, and was staring at me intently all the time. As at lunch, I couldn't understand why Ted and Patrizia didn't notice this. We saw a gun hanging over a wide bed in a room that smelt of sweat. I longed to get back to the warm brightness of the big kitchen, away from these claustrophobic rooms that looked somehow familiar to me, as if I had seen them in a dream. I turned around and saw with horror that Ted and Patrizia weren't there. I could hear them talking and laughing in the hallway, where they had lingered to look at a picture. I was alone with Michele. I turned back. His face was inches from mine.

I don't remember what happened next, which is probably just as well. They must have carried me out of the house, for I remember coming to on the front step. I cried and clung to Ted, and I'll never forget how embarrassed everyone was, particularly me, as the initial shock began to wear off. Everyone was keen to explain it away, I was tired, I was *nervosa*, I was so sensitive that all that blood and offal had been more than I could take.

A second meal had been prepared in the kitchen, not as large as the first, but still more than enough. This time Michele sat beside Patrizia, and I was left in peace to pick at a bit of cold meat and some salad. The evening trailed on, because in Italy people find it hard to say goodbye, and so they extend the day for as long as is possible. After dinner, somebody pulled out a pack of cards. I sat by the fire with Franca while Ted tried to learn the rules of some complicated four-hand game, but even the cards, with their suits of sticks and cups were strange to him. He partnered Lucia, and she pretended to be furious as he lost trick after trick on them, until they eventually lost the game.

When the time did come for us to leave, it was a slow parting because there were so many of us, and everybody had to be said goodbye to individually. They told us to come again, to come back at Easter when the hams we had seen being prepared that day would be ready to eat. Ted wanted to drive my car back but I insisted that it would be no problem for me, and a sleepy Lucia directed us down the twists and bends of the road, back to S. Giorgio.

13

I had a dream about snow. I often had nightmares about cold things, such as being trapped in an icy wasteland, the land and the sky both mercilessly white. You couldn't see where one ended and the other began, and for some reason that was terrible. Another time I dreamt that I was trapped in a cathedral which was for some odd reason packed with ice. Stranger still, I was perched at the top of an ugly baroque altar of rotting wood. Far below me, I could see the huge green ice-bergs drift menacingly through the nave. It was a foolish dream, but it still left me with a feeling of terror when I awoke.

This cold dream, a dream of snow, that I had at the end of January was also very strange. It was one of those dreams that is particularly convincing because it begins with you dreaming that you're in bed asleep – which of course you are, so that whatever happens next seems logical and real. So, I dreamt that I was lying in bed sleeping, in the apartment in S. Giorgio, in the middle of the night, when the roof of the building suddenly rolled back without a sound. The bare sky was above me, and it was snowing. I knew all this, even though I was still lying with my eyes closed, and believed myself to be sleeping. The snowfall was heavy, and it drifted down on me where I lay. It quietly swallowed up things on the floor: a book I had been reading before I went to sleep the night before and had put on the bedside rug, a pair of shoes, a wastepaper-basket. It came up the side of the cupboard. I was aware that it was now as deep as my bed was high. The surface of the snow was level with me where I lay, and still it fell. I began to feel very frightened. There was a chill layer over my face and hair. That was one thing, but I knew that I would have to wake up if I was to save myself from being buried alive. The snow kept falling. I was still lying there, and part of me wanted to stay sleeping, to succumb to the soft, deadly coldness, while the rest of me knew that I must resist. By now the snow was piled deep upon me, the whiteness was giving way to darkness, to an uncompromising black. I was on the point of surrendering to the inevitable when I woke up, not in a bed buried in snow, but in my dry, soundly roofed room. I felt completely devastated.

A short while later I was standing in Adolfo's bar, licking sugar and jam from my fingers, calling for a second coffee. There was, of course, no snow in S. Giorgio that morning: it wasn't even a particularly cold day. It was mild all over Europe that year, but even during the hardest winter, S. Giorgio doesn't get much snow. Where I grew up in County Clare it hardly ever snowed, and when it did, it never lay on the ground but melted away at once. I always liked to look at the snow falling. One night, my father called me to the front door when I was on my way to bed. 'Look,' he said, 'the Old Lady is plucking geese up in Greenland and throwing down the feathers.' I looked up and I saw them. The big soft wet flakes fell out of the blackness into the light above the door, but for me they were feathers, not snow. There really was an old woman at the top of the world, throwing down a million feathers: my father told me so, and I believed him.

It was a Monday morning. I didn't like to start the week badly, and I hoped to shake off the gloom of the nightmare and salvage the rest of the morning. My luck, however, was out. When I pulled into the forecourt of the factory, I saw that Fabiola's big red car was already parked there. I swore out loud when I saw it. I wasn't in the mood to talk to her, in fact I didn't feel like talking to anyone. I just wanted to get to my desk and start work, but to do that, I had to go through Pietro's office, where I knew Fabiola would be. When I went in, there she was, sitting behind Pietro's desk arguing with him, while he leaned against a filing cabinet with a sheaf of papers in his hand and a harassed expression on his face. When Fabiola saw me, she jumped up and kissed me, enveloping me in her familiar scent of perfume and fur. She was still tanned from her holidays, and I asked her if she had enjoyed the Seychelles. She looked sideways at Pietro and then said, 'Oh, it was all right, I suppose. A beach is a beach, after all, it's the same everywhere.' She didn't ask me how my trip to Venice had been: I didn't expect her to.

'Travel is wonderful, though, isn't it,' she said as soon as Pietro went out of the room. 'I'm already thinking about where to go this summer. I'm so pleased about all these changes in the Communist countries, because now it'll be safe to go there. I've heard that Prague is very pretty. Who knows? We might even go to Russia.'

Fabiola had travelled more than probably anyone else I knew, but it amounted to strangely little with her. She went abroad at least twice a year, and visited European cities like Amsterdam and Paris, as well as more distant places, such as Kenya and Canada. However, she travelled in such luxury and with such a lack of curiosity that afterwards it would all become a blur in her mind of four-star hotels and first-class restaurants. She would forget where she had been, and nothing remained but vague images. A few years before she met me, she had been to Ireland on a Castles and Gardens tour, but with the exception of 'Dublino', where she had spent a couple of nights, she couldn't remember the name of a single place she had visited there. I tried to jog her memory with a few names.

'Did you go to Killarney?' but she only furrowed her brow and said, 'Perhaps. I don't know. I really don't remember now.' She could describe nothing she had seen other than 'some castles that had been turned into hotels, and the countryside was very green'.

And yet, the oddest thing of all was that she had a dream of visiting a place where Pietro resolutely refused to take her. Above all other cities in the world, Fabiola longed to visit Calcutta.

'It must be so wonderful there,' she said to me dreamily. I said nothing. She had rendered me speechless. Fabiola was the sort of woman it took a leap of imagination to picture pushing a trolley full of cabbages and toilet rolls up and down the aisle of a supermarket, let alone standing in the streets of Calcutta. 'They call it the City of Palaces you know. I read an article about it once, it said that there is a great sense of joy there. Of course the people have very little, but they probably have a deep spiritual belief, and I'm sure they're very happy. But I still can't talk Pietro into going there.' Fabiola probably didn't realize that the Calcutta Holiday Inn didn't exist, that it couldn't, that it was a contradiction in terms.

'You're lucky, Aisling,' she said. 'You're free, you can go absolutely anywhere you want.' I knew she would think it poor form of me to point out that there was one other prerequisite besides freedom for travel: money. I had had to take on a lot of extra work for the trip I was planning to America. I used to get irritated by her refusal to acknowledge the economic difference there was between us. She was always telling me that she had seen just the coat for me, at a price I could never afford, or that I should take myself off ski-ing in the middle of winter when my bank account was still recovering from Christmas, or that I go to some overpriced restaurant near Assisi where they had the most wonderful *spaghetti ai tartufi neri*.

Pietro put his head round the door, and told me that there was a fax just in from London, and could I come and look at it please? 'Aisling's talking to me,' Fabiola said grandly. 'She'll come when she's ready.' Pietro scowled and mumbled, but retreated back to the main office. It was extraordinary how she had him under her thumb. I was glad he had come in though, and a couple of minutes later, I made my excuses. She swept her fur around her and left, in search of some other distraction to fill what was left of her morning.

What was left of mine went quickly enough, with so much work that I didn't notice the time passing. As I was going home from work at lunch time, for some reason I remembered that a local archaeologist had told me that the road along which I was now driving had once been a Roman road. Some excavations had been carried out there, and many of the Roman artifacts in S. Giorgio's museum had been found there. The archaeologist said she thought that there were still probably many things buried in that area, and added that if you looked at the state of museums in Italy, it was probably better if the artifacts remained under the ground. Mosaics, painting, pottery, frescoes, Roman stonework and statues, from the most sublime art to objects whose sole interest and virtue lay in their antiquity: it was hard for the imagination to grasp the sheer quantity of such things in Italy. The Italians had neither the means, nor, more importantly, the will to properly maintain and restore their heritage. Given the weight of Italian history, the wonder of it was that it sat so lightly on the people, now speeding past in their cars. I imagined that I was looking at the scene from a great height, and saw not just the traffic, but the bones, the jewellery and the shards of broken pottery that were buried under the soil, and I felt a sudden rush of pity for everything that had ever been.

The following Saturday I went to Siena with Ted, and on the way there I mentioned to him what the archaeologist had told me. He agreed. 'The more you hear about Italian museums,' he said, 'the more you wonder.' He told me the worst story he'd ever heard was from a woman he knew who worked in a state museum in Florence, who once visited a gallery in Naples while on holiday. When the attendant there found out that she also worked in a state museum, in a spirit of fellowship he picked three little squares of glass out of a Roman mosaic in his keeping, and gallantly presented them to her as a souvenir.

It was quite a while since I had been to Siena. It was a city I liked, although my initial impression of it had been bad. My first trip to Siena had been years ago, on my first visit to Italy. I had liked the art and the architecture, but the general atmosphere of the city unsettled me. The people I dealt with in shops and restaurants struck me as cold and closed in a manner which was something more than the usual result of excessive exposure to tourists.

Then one afternoon, I went into a bookshop and casually picked up what I thought was an art magazine. It had a glossy innocuous cover with an abstract painting on it, but when I opened it, I found that it was full of violent pornographic cartoons. There were drawings of live women being cut open, women having their backs broken, naked women being led along by nooses around their necks. Sickened and disgusted, I closed the magazine, and for a long time I damned Siena with that. It was years before I realized that it wasn't exceptional to see such stuff for sale in Italy, nor for it to be beside art books, with no differentiation between the two. As far as the people who ran the shops were concerned, they were all just things to be sold. It would be hard to find a news-stand anywhere there which did not have a huge stock of magazines even more violent and fearful than the one I saw. And this of course was another of the things which was never acknowledged abroad, because it would have spoiled the myth of Italy as a passionate country, as a place of sexual freedom and happiness.

When we arrived in Siena we went straight to the main picture gallery, and I don't think I've ever seen Ted happier than he was that day, as we walked around looking at the paintings. For a long time it was a bit of a mystery to me why he loved early religious art so much. Then I realized that people often like what you wouldn't expect, and that you can tell a lot about someone by the sort of painting they prefer. For instance, I was amazed when I read somewhere that Raphael was Dostoevsky's favourite artist. The painting he loved most of all was the Sistine Madonna. He had a copy of it, and towards the end of his life he would sit gazing at it for long periods of time, lost in contemplation. I don't like the Sistine Madonna: I think it's far too sweet and mawkish, like a lot of Raphael's religious paintings. When Dostoevsky was in Basel, on his way through to Italy, he saw Holbein's painting of the dead Christ. It made a tremendous impression on him, and he never forgot it. It shows Christ as a dead man, after he had been taken from the cross, his body already beginning to decompose. There is no sense of divinity, no sense of anything but death. Dostoyevsky said that looking at it could cause a man to lose his faith. I could understand the significance which the Holbein had for him more easily than the Raphael. There was a strain of sentimentality in Dostoevsky which didn't interest me, and which I didn't wish to acknowledge, but I couldn't deny it was there, when I thought of the Sistine Madonna.

What Raphael meant to Dostoevsky was one thing: what Simone Martini meant to Ted was another matter entirely. Until that day, there was something about his attitude to art that didn't quite add up for me. For one thing, I couldn't understand why he had no time for modern or contemporary art. The more recent it was, the less interest he had. There was a big retrospective of Andy Warhol in Venice that year, and he didn't want to go to see it, he sneered at the very idea. There was nothing inherently wrong in this, no reason why he should prefer Pop Art to Sienese painting of the early Renaissance. But I could see how necessary the forms of twentieth-century art were, and how they had had to come into existence to express the way people thought now, how they lived, how they saw things: in short, to express how the world was now. I could see this more clearly than most, because I wasn't a part of it. Human nature may have changed around 1910, but there are still a few places where it hasn't changed yet, or is only now beginning to change. Where I grew up in Ireland was one such place. I used to think that if I had known this earlier, it might have saved me a lot of pain, but now I wasn't so sure.

I think perhaps other people thought I couldn't see the difference that there was between me and them: people in Italy, Ted, or Bill, the man I'd known in Paris. They could certainly see it, and I think that such friends as I had liked me for that difference, which they saw as an old-worldliness, which looked eccentric, and at times more than slightly ridiculous. It shows itself in small but significant ways. Sometimes when I go to visit people, I bake a cake and bring it to them. When I have dinner at someone's house, I always write them a thank-you note afterwards. It took me years to get over the idea of having good clothes set aside for special occasions, a hangover from the 'Sunday best' mentality. In Paris once, someone I knew had a baby, and I knitted a little jumper for it. She was so staggered when I gave it to her, that I've never dared to do it again, not even for Jimmy's kids. As I say, these things are small, but I know better than anybody that they indicate a mind-set far from the common run in the late twentieth century.

I suppose it would have been funny, if it hadn't been so painful, and finding out that everyone was playing life by different rules than the ones I'd been told were valid was very painful. I've never been promiscuous. That American I knew in Paris was the first man I'd been to bed with, and when he left me, I found it hard not to think that the lacerating pain and the rage I felt were not divine retribution for my sin, even though I knew that this was a reprehensible and cowardly attitude. One thing I really admired in contemporary society was the attempt to develop an adult morality, that is, a desire to do right for its own sake, rather than from fear of being punished by God. If I had ever seen this new mature morality working in practice rather than just in theory, I'm sure I would have admired it even more.

I've always believed that the big difference was that Ireland hadn't been involved in the Second World War, so that we didn't undergo that necessary period of nihilism; a loss of faith not just in God but in all authority. To some extent we also missed out on that rampant materialism that had spread all over Europe, and which still astounded me, even after having lived in the middle of it for years. While Ted stood rapt before the paintings I eyed the other people wandering around the gallery. There was a young couple beside us with a video camera and a guidebook, comfortable shoes, and expensive, bright casual clothes. They looked indistinguishable from any number of people I'd seen in the past, tourists in Florence, S. Giorgio, Rome. The woman's face wore a slightly puzzled, slightly anxious expression. The man's face was blank. I wondered what on earth they saw in all these gilt Madonnas, stern saints and stiffly holy angels. When we went into the next room, the only other person there was a gallery attendant, slumped in his chair asleep, and snoring unashamedly.

'What have you got against contemporary painting, anyway?' I said peevishly all of a sudden. Ted was a bit taken aback at both the question and the tone, but he answered immediately, 'It won't last. It's incoherent.'

'And you think the twentieth century isn't?'

'It is, of course. That's the problem. The art being made now is completely unlike the art of any other period in the whole history of humanity, because everything is different now. There's never been a period like this.'

'And don't you think that's exciting?' I said.

'No, Aisling, I don't, I think it's depressing. There's a sort of madness now. Look, if you take say, this painting here,' and he indicated Ambrogio Lorenzetti's tiny picture of a walled town by the sea, 'and, say, a Vermeer, an African Mask and a Japanese print, even though they're all from such different eras and cultures you can see at once that they have something in common. The same things have always mattered to people, things like love and death, and though they may use completely different forms to express them, the fears and desires are the same, which is why the meaning of a work of art can transcend its own period and place. But if you look at the things being made now, well, I truly believe that they will be interesting in the future only to show how crazy a time this was. It'll be beyond belief, Aisling. They'll wonder what ever possessed us. What we call art will only look ugly and stupid.'

'So you mean they won't last because they're not pleasant to look at? Because they're not decorative?'

'No, because they're not beautiful.'

'Lots of them are beautiful.'

'Well then, because they're not sublime.'

'I don't know what you mean by sublime.'

'Oh Aisling,' he said, and he looked at me shrewdly, in a way he'd never looked at me before, 'I think that you do.'

I still wasn't convinced. 'There used to be a sense of wholeness,' he said. 'That's gone now.'

'Do you think I don't know that?'

I was tempted to dismiss Ted as a philistine with a sentimental streak and a fondness for paintings that looked like what they were supposed to be, but as soon as this thought came to my mind, I had to dismiss it. I knew it was unfair and untrue. Rather, he could somehow reach beyond things he didn't believe in, and get at their truth. I found that hard to understand.

On leaving the gallery, we walked back towards the centre of town, went up Banche di Sopra, and had a glass of Chianti and a ham roll for lunch in Nannini's. Ted commented on the extraordinary prices of the bottles of vintage Brunello di Montalcino displayed on the mirrored shelves behind the bar, and I bought a slab of white nougat studded with pistachios to take back to Franca. All the time we were in the bar, though, I was still pursuing the same line of thought from the morning in the gallery. I was more conscious than ever before of the difference – and the distance – between Ted and me. I looked across at him as he tried to engage a frosty waitress in conversation as she made him a coffee. He didn't seem to mind that she wasn't responding. Sometimes when I looked at him in a public situation like this I saw him as someone I knew and to whom I felt very close, and then when I looked again, he was a stranger. When that happened, I was particularly aware of his being from an anonymous society. That made him as he was, and I wasn't like that at all. I remembered how we talked about our childhoods one night, and then we had talked about religion. He said his parents had taken him to church now and then when he was a child, but he had always known that their hearts weren't in it. They were doing it because they felt they ought to, not out of any sort of belief. They had all been glad when they'd been able to drop the pretence and stop going.

'Anyway,' Ted had said to me, 'we were Lutheran, and I've really grown to dislike that. I think Protestantism misses the whole point of Christianity completely. There are lots of things I don't like about Catholicism either, but from having lived in Italy I understand it more and I like it more. Here, Catholicism fits because it's a Mediterranean religion. All that talk in the Bible about olive groves and vineyards and fish, that makes sense to me here. You drink a good wine in Italy, and you see why Christ wanted to make a sacrament out of it. Then you have these churches in the north of Europe and America and they're so afraid of life, they give you a thimbleful of grape juice, and then pride themselves on their own self-righteousness. Religion interests me in terms of its relation to a given society, and of course above all in its connections with art, but that's as far as it goes, and as far as I want it to go. The idea of faith doesn't interest me at all.'

My own experience had been so different. I couldn't think of my childhood without thinking of the religion which had been an integral part of it. Everything about it caught my imagination, from the idea that I had a guardian angel (whom I longed to catch unawares and therefore visible) to our parish church with its fake grotto. I had a little plastic shrine I was particularly fond of, because the statue was in a niche behind a pair of tiny gates, and I liked the secretness of that, liked how you could close over the gates, and then the statue would be hidden. Every spring, the nuns at school encouraged us to make a May altar: not that I needed any encouragement. I loved going through the fields to gather flowers at dusk, and then I'd put them in two jars and set up my plastic shrine on a clean cloth, with a candle before it. I made the mistake of telling Ted about it, trying to describe how much the final effect had pleased me, with the scent of the flowers and the soft light of the candle. He thought this was the strangest thing: if I'd told this anecdote in connection with my grandmother I think he'd have coped with that, but he couldn't believe that my own childhood had been so antediluvian. Half charmed and half shocked, he had wanted to know more, but I had quickly changed the subject.

Again I wondered what it was we had in common, and why we were together. The following month we would go to the States together, and even though I was looking forward to it, there were also moments when I dreaded it. We were to stay some of the time with his family, and I was afraid of what I would know there, about him and about myself. Yet I was still so old-fashioned that I couldn't stop believing that this self-knowledge was one of the most important things you could have in life.

As he was finishing his coffee Ted said, 'Let's go see the *Maestà* in the cathedral museum after lunch, then go over the road to the cathedral itself. Is that OK?' I said that was fine.

When we left Nannini's, it was raining. On our way to the museum, we passed a gap between two buildings on the left, where a flight of steps led down to Piazza Del Campo. 'It's funny if you're here in the summer,' I said, 'you can hardly get down those steps because of the crowds of people that are always standing there taking photos of the square. It's strange to see.'

I had seen Duccio's *Maestà* several times before. When we went into the room in the museum where it is exhibited, there were about twenty people sitting before the main panel. A guide was talking to them in French, and I idly listened in as she told them how the painting had originally been above the main altar of Siena cathedral. I thought it a pity that it wasn't still there. In the room where it now hung temperature and humidity could be controlled, but I always think you lose so much when you can't see a painting in its original context. Even the best lose something when they're moved, and minor works gain too from being seen where they belong. Ted and I were standing at the back of the room, where the paintings of the predella were displayed. Ted whispered to me, 'You know that the whole thing isn't here, don't you? Some of the panels are in the States. Maybe you'll get to see them when we go to Washington.'

I looked across the room again, and tried to imagine how the whole thing would look if it were to be put together again, and replaced above the main altar of the cathedral: the tiny exquisite panels showing scenes from the life of Christ under and around the vast central panel, with its lovely Madonna and child, and the ranks of angels which surrounded them. I tried to imagine the effect of candlelight on all that gold, and how the eyes of the angels would look. The guide was telling the group of how the painting had been broken up, and they gasped lightly when she pointed out where the main panel had been sawn into pieces. I turned back to the predella, and looked at one scene in particular, showing 'The Washing of The Feet'. I looked deep into it, and I tried to see it as it was when it was made. I was trying now not to re-create in my mind the form of the original, but to see the meaning of it, to enter as fully as possible into its original spirit. And then I realized that I couldn't do it, any more than Ted could. I was conscious of the huge construction of theology and iconography which no longer had any relevance for me, but which informed every inch of the *Maestà*. The Madonna was beautiful, as beautiful as Aphrodite. I thought of the paintings I'd seen that morning in the gallery, and now I saw them all in the same way, like magnificent images painted on doors to the past that were shut and locked. I thought of the plastic shrine I'd had as a child. The memory of it still meant something to me, because it was ugly but simple, and what I had lost while looking at the *Maestà* was faith in all things that weren't simple. I couldn't relate the painting to faith any more, and I couldn't relate the shrine to anything else.

When we were on the train to Florence that evening, I looked at the sky and thought of being in the cathedral some hours earlier. I'd seen a young man there chewing gum and blowing it into pink, sticky bubbles as he looked, unmoved, at the pulpit. Suddenly I realized how much I was looking forward to going to America, because I longed to be away, if only a while, from the weight of the past.

14

Ted and I left for America early one morning in February. I felt excited and nervous as we waited with our luggage to check in for the flight: excited because I like travelling, nervous because it's as if airports are custom built to make you feel that way. Say what you like, flying is deeply unnatural, and everybody knows that, from the heads of airlines down to people who won't set foot on a plane.

As if he were reading my thoughts, Ted suddenly remarked, 'Airports are weird,' as we walked away from the check-in desk. 'I can never figure out why they have to feel so different to train stations.' The departure area was so crowded that we decided to go straight through passport control and security, and wait on the other side until it was time to board our flight. When all the formalities were over, Ted bought himself a coffee and sat down to read the paper, while I wandered off to have a look at the shops. I hadn't the slightest interest in doing so, but we were going to be cooped up beside each other the whole way across the Atlantic, so I thought it would be good if we had at least half an hour on our own before the journey began.

I was glad to see that Ted was so relaxed and happy, and looking forward to being back in America for a while. He didn't seem unduly troubled about having me as a travelling companion, although I had tried to warn him that I might be difficult. He had heard me out, then said mildly, 'Oh, I know that, Aisling. You can be hell in your own apartment, never mind at thirty thousand feet above the Atlantic. I don't expect you to be any worse or better than you usually are,' which didn't please me as much as I think he thought it would. 'What about your parents?' I asked, and he said, 'Oh, they'll think you're just as sweet as you can be.' Ted's more ironic than your average American. I let the matter drop at that.

This trip to America would be the longest period of time we'd ever spent together, and travel can strain a relationship like nothing else. I really had done my best to warn him beforehand, and recounted a couple of new, gruesome dreams, to which he listened with interest, but without comment. Anyway, I thought, if I did crack up completely while I was away, at least he couldn't say that I'd deceived him about how things were.

I mooched about the Duty Free area for a while, but I didn't buy anything. I never do when I'm flying. I'm always put off by the excess, the greed you see in Duty Free shops; all the bottles and packets and even the bars of chocolate on sale are much bigger than normal. It's like the airlines want you to wallow in greed while you're waiting, to take your mind off the fact that you might never get to where you're going. They make these big glittery shops, and then fill them with things that give you the most stereotypical view of the country: blue and white delft in Amsterdam; linen in Dublin. This being Italy, there was high fashion on sale, and a lot of food: wine, hams and expensive coloured pasta. It was still too soon to go back to Ted, so I walked up and down looking at the departure gates, and the groups of people waiting at each one. There was a flight due to leave for Ankara, and I noticed a particular Turkish family group who were waiting for it. They were sitting on the floor, probably because the wire benches in the departure lounge of Fiumicino are so uncomfortable, and they were eating a meal of large, crudely made sandwiches wrapped in tinfoil. People were looking at them with open contempt and suspicion, because they were Turkish and poor, because they didn't blend in with their slick surroundings, and they didn't seem to care.

When I got back to Ted, he had finished his coffee, and was folding up his newspaper. We went together to the departure gate, and went down a tube, into the plane. As in the airport, there was that same feeling of induced alienation that makes me feel so uneasy. The stewardesses went through the usual

138

charade with the lifejackets and the oxygen masks, to which no one paid the slightest attention. We taxied into line behind three other planes, and then we saw each of them in turn speed down the runway. Our turn came, and as we gathered speed, they played a quick blast of bland music. The flat yellow and brown fields fell away below us. The music was cut off as abruptly as it had been started, and a few moments later, the seatbelt signs blipped off.

We were flying to New York and from there we were to get a connection down to Washington, where Ted's family lived, and where we were to spend the first week. The cabin crew brought us a meal as we crossed the Alps. Looking down we could see the snow on the tops of the serene, inhuman mountains, and the tiny villages strung out along the bottom of the deep valleys. I found it hard to imagine people down there, as the inhabitants of the villages no doubt found it hard to believe that there were over a hundred people having breakfast in the speck of silver that they could see moving across a bare sky.

I love the sky. When countries try to encourage people to visit them, they always cite the most obvious things: the sunshine, the food, the museums and monuments. They never suggest how good it might be just to smell a different air, or to see a new sky, and how strange and beautiful that could be. I always thought the summer sky in Italy to be over-rated. It was too empty, too high and featureless, too bald and blue, with a fierce sun in it. I think Ireland must have one of the loveliest skies in the world, I could sit and look at an Atlantic sky for hours on end, watching the marvellous clouds, the way you can look into a fire and never feel bored. I like to imagine the world from far away, the atmosphere surrounding it like a pearly skin. And then I think of that skin seen from the inside, with all the variable skies drifting imperceptibly into each other, changing as landscape changes when you travel through it. The sky is timeless, unlike the weathered stone of buildings or paintings that fade. You can look at the sky and after an hour it's already different, but because of that it can look the same after a thousand years. The sky is as ancient as the sea, and I love them both for that.

'Are you nervous?' Ted suddenly asked me, taking my hand. I said that I was, just a little. There was no point in lying, because he could read my moods so well that it was hardly worth his while to ask me, and a lie would only have confused the issue. 'But I'm happy too,' I said. 'I'm looking forward to the States.'

'Well you should,' he said, 'because you're going to have a ball.'

I started enjoying America even before we landed there, some eight hours later. As the plane was descending to the airport, we could already see the buildings below, when suddenly I knew we were flying over Manhattan, because the buildings bristled up below unexpectedly, and you knew to look at them that it was the immense height of the sky-scrapers that made this effect, not that the plane was flying lower.

As we went through customs, I felt glad about so many things: glad Ted was with me, glad *somebody* was with me, glad that I was only there for a holiday, that I spoke the language, that I had enough money. The official who checked my passport seemed disappointed that it was completely in order. He stamped it, then slammed it down on the counter with real violence.

The air was bitterly cold when we went outside to wait for a transfer bus to La Guardia. The darkening sky was full of planes, some taking off, some coming in to land. The coldness was a shock after the dried-out artificial air and the warmth of the plane and the airport. It was already dark when we got to La Guardia. When we boarded the Washington plane, we were ignored by the stewardesses, who were standing in a cluster gossiping about a difficult passenger on the preceding flight. I was glad they left us alone: they looked a bit frightening to me. The stewardesses looked oddly similar, as if they were made up to play sisters in a film. They were all very tall, with heaped blonde hair and an air of hard confidence. As the plane taxied, the stewardesses went through the safety drill, and once we were in the air, they moved through the plane doling out cans of Coke and bags of honeyroast peanuts.

Looking out of the window I saw Manhattan, as recognizable

as it was unexpected, neat as a map, the lights glittering along its grids of streets. Ted said he'd never seen it so clearly before, even though he'd flown in and out of New York many times.

'Do you think I'll like New York?' I asked him. 'Oh, it's hard to say. I hope you do, but there's no way of knowing.' Generally I like cities. I like how you can feel hidden in them. It was a bit similar to how I felt about my job in the factory. I liked being a small part in the whole process of making and selling things, and in the city, you can feel small and insignificant, but know that you're still a part of the life of the city. It can be comforting to blend with the crowd.

If, when we arrived in Washington, I had had to get on yet another plane and sit there for another four hours, I would have done it uncomplainingly. It wasn't because I was enjoying the journey, but because I was so weary that I wouldn't have had the energy to resist. By the time we were dragging our suitcases off the carousel, I felt like a piece of luggage myself. Ted's father met us. He looked like an older version of Ted, and he hugged us both. His mother hugged me too, when we arrived at the house about an hour later. I don't remember much about that first night there. His mother gave me some milk and biscuits, and I remember seeing a big orange cat stalking across the carpet. After that, I went to bed and fell into a solid sleep and I remember that I didn't dream at all.

When I woke up the next morning, for a split second I had that feeling of complete disorientation that you can have on waking in a strange place. Then I became aware of Ted's mother's voice through the floor-boards, and remembered where I was. It sounded like she was talking to herself, because her voice was the only one I could hear. When I went downstairs, I found that Ted and his father were also in the kitchen with her, mildly putting a word in edgeways when they had a chance. The big ginger cat I had seen the night before was sitting on Ted's lap. Everybody else had been up long before me, and the pot of coffee sitting on the kitchen table was stone cold. I thought they might make a fresh pot, and I was a bit surprised when Ted's mother just poured some of the old coffee into a mug for me, and then put it in the microwave to heat up. Ted nudged the cat on to the floor, and made me some toast.

Over breakfast, I tried to watch Ted's mother out of the corner of my eye, to get the measure of her, but I had to abandon that before long, because I found that she was doing exactly the same thing to me. She won that little war of nerves, as I suspect she was used to doing. I was very interested in her, because I always think you can tell a lot about a man by looking at his mother.

I felt from the first that I'd probably met my match in Ted's mother ('Call me Susan,' she'd said when Ted first introduced us). I don't know what I'd expected her to be like, but I certainly hadn't foreseen this tiny powerhouse: incessant, nervous and manipulative in a way that only another manipulator can detect. Yet she was gentle too, and vulnerable. I kept thinking of what Ted had told me about his grandmother, and I could see the effect she'd had on Susan. She was never able to stop and relax, because she always felt that something was expected of her by those around her. As small as I am, and slight, almost frail in build, Susan was soft-spoken, but made up in quantity for what she lacked in volume. While Ted, his father, ('Hi, I'm Bob,' he'd said simply) and I sat quietly at the table that morning, I watched her move restlessly round the kitchen, getting muffins out of a bag for me, taking a two-quart jar of cranapple juice out of the fridge and pouring a glass for Ted, and talking, talking, talking all the time.

'Now, Ted, the very first thing I want you to do this morning is to start clearing out all those boxes.' Ted groaned quietly. He had told me before we arrived that he had lots of things in his parents' attic to clear out: 'A mountain of junk,' was how he'd cheerfully described it to me. His mother had written to him threatening to throw it all away if he didn't come back and sort it out. The primary reason for his trip was that the college he taught at in Florence was affiliated to a private college in Washington, whose students had the option of going to Italy for a semester or for a year. He needed to see the head of the college to talk about some plans and improvements for the programme he taught. While he was in the States, he was going to sort out the things he'd left there. 'I'm glad to have the opportunity,' he'd said to me. 'There comes a time in everyone's life to throw things away, and for me that time is now.' I thought that was a good enough reason in itself to cross the Atlantic. There wasn't much left belonging to me in the house back in Clare, but there were some things, perhaps more than I cared to remember, and I thought that maybe sometime soon I'd get round to going home and doing the same thing as Ted.

I remembered how we'd once seen something in a newspaper about a hurricane in America, and Ted had remarked, 'I think my Mom would be happy if the house was hit by a hurricane. She'd see it as a challenge to put the whole thing back together again.' Now I understood what he'd meant. She wanted the attic cleared, because during the summer it was to be converted into an extra bedroom. 'It'll add so much to the value of the house,' she said. There were already two spare bedrooms, a guest bathroom and a dining room which was never used. I also could understand now why Ted's mother wasn't interested in religion. Nothing that was spiritual or internalized interested her. For Susan, life was a series of external problems, connected with money and things: food, clothes, property. In the past, life had obligingly provided a wealth of these problems: children to be fed and dressed, a home to be made. But now everything was finished and complete, and so she was forced to create things for herself to do, such as this unnecessary attic conversion. Inside her, there was nothing but pure driven will, but she wasn't aware of it, because she never thought about herself in this way. She had already planned the décor for the new room, and pulled out some thick books of swatches and samples to show us what she'd chosen. Her husband sneaked out of the room while she was busy with this, Uncle Silas the cat at his heels.

Bob reminded me of one of those trees you see in the West of Ireland, where the prevailing winds blow in off the Atlantic, and the tree grows completely flattened, all its branches pointing due East. He'd lived in the full blast of Susan's willpower for nigh on half a century, and had yielded to it decades ago. If a genie had given him a wish, he'd have asked to be made invisible. In

143

the absence of genies, he'd worked hard on the next-best thing: complete self-effacement. He was a sweet-natured man, and reminded me a lot of Ted. Later in the day he showed me his room with an air of shy delight, like a child telling you a secret.

'Susan says I'm lazy because I spend so much time in here reading,' he said. 'As far as she's concerned, books are just a waste of time. Sometimes I say to her, "I have nothing else to do these days, so I might as well read." But she replies, "Well, I'm sure if you looked hard, you would find something to do." Truth is, I don't look hard. I don't look at all. I like my books too much,' and he indicated the shelves neatly lined with volumes relating mostly to the Second World War and scientific subjects. The room was high and bright. As well as the books, there was a television, a stereo, and a comfortable-looking armchair. On the floor by the chair was a beanbag covered in cotton printed with fishbones, where the cat was curled up asleep. 'Uncle Silas keeps me company, don't you?' said Bob, and the cat at once lifted its head knowingly.

'Now what can I play for you, Aisling?' said Bob, crossing to the stereo. 'What sort of music do you like? I'm afraid I don't have anything recent, all my albums are probably too old to appeal to you.' He started to rummage through his record collection. 'This is a good one, I think you'll like this. I haven't listened to this one for a long time myself. Do you have Glenn Miller in Ireland? This brings back a lot of memories for me, of the time when Susan and I were young and just starting out together, like you and Ted.'

As soon as these words were out, Bob was covered in confusion. 'That's not to say you and Ted will – I mean, it's not to say that you won't, either . . .' We were both embarrassed, and both grateful for the swell of plaintive music that suddenly filled the room, and allowed us to fall silent. Bob lit a cigarette and drew on it deeply. I smiled and said, 'It doesn't matter.' He smiled back, grateful and relieved.

During the following days, Ted went to the college every morning. He dropped me off on the way there, most often at The Mall, and I visited the Vietnam Memorial and the National

Gallery. Ted would meet me in the middle of the day and we'd have lunch, then we'd visit a museum or a gallery together.

On the third day, we went to the National Museum of Air and Space. For me, its greatest impact came from the size of the things it contained, and the amount of money you knew had been involved in putting them there (although it must be said that these were exactly the same factors that impressed me about the contents of Susan's fridge). The main hall was large enough to contain several small aeroplanes and the nose cone of a rocket, yet it still seemed airy and spacious. It made me feel queasy to look at the nose cone, with its scorched surface. The compartments where the astronauts had sat while travelling back to earth were so tiny, it must have felt like they were coming back from the moon in the boot of a car.

'Have you ever seen the moon dust in the Vatican?' I asked Ted. He said that he hadn't. I told him that in the Vatican Museums, as well as the Fra Angelico Chapel and Raphael's fresco of the School of Athens, there's also some moon dust, and a tiny Papal flag, said to have gone to the moon and back the first time the Americans went there. 'There's a card in front of them that says they were a gift to the Pope from President Nixon,' I said. Ted thought this was hilarious. 'If Nixon gave you a little bit of dirt and said it was moon dust, would you believe him?' One of the things I like about the Vatican Museums is that mixture of sublime art and old junk: all the stuff you know the Cardinals feel obliged to hang on to, in case the Head of State who gave it to them ever comes calling again. So you look at this tiny flag and you know it's been to the moon and back, and in one way that's extraordinary, and then you think again, and it's the most absurd thing you've ever heard. It means nothing: the ultimate big deal.

From the first, I took a flip attitude to the Air and Space Museum, and I was surprised to see that this annoyed Ted. I thought the whole place was something other than what it pretended to be. He didn't see it that way at all, and thought I should have been more impressed than I was with the complicated toys and models demonstrating various scientific proofs and principles. It wasn't designed to inform, but to stun.

There was a cinema in the museum, where we saw a short movie about space exploration called *The Dream Is Alive*. The screen was massive, and one's senses were put under such heavy visual and auditory bombardment that while it lasted, it was hard to do anything as mundane as think. We saw pictures of the earth taken from space. I think people around me, including Ted, were a bit put out when I began to snigger, but it was more than I could do to stop myself as Walter Cronkite boomed over an image of the Mediterranean: 'Greece: cradle of our civilization.' I sniggered again when it showed shots of a rocket taking off, and all the men in mission control punched the air with clenched fists. It was as subtle as one of those Italian ads when they show a bottle of *spumante* being opened, and all the foam gushes down the sides. It didn't say anything at all about the military implications, but we saw some cute pictures of bees that had been taken into space to see if they could make honey in zero gravity conditions, as if the whole point of the space programme was to make extra-terrestrial honey, and provide weird souvenirs for the Pope.

I laughed, but the final effect of the visit was to depress me, as did Washington cathedral, which we saw afterwards. I hated its twentieth-century gothic, its ersatz oldness. On the way home, we stopped at a Chinese restaurant, and bought four meals to go. By the time we got back to the house, the sweet-and-sour pork and the stir-fried rice were cold, so Susan heated them up in the microwave. She ate with Ted and me at the kitchen table, surrounded by the wreckage of cardboard cartons in which the food had come. Bob put his dinner on a tray, and took it off to eat in his room, where he had been watching a programme on television about the possible reunification of Germany.

'I don't get it,' he said, standing with his tray in his hands. 'I just don't get it. How can Europe even begin to think of allowing Germany to get big again? Has everybody over there forgotten what it was like the last time? I haven't forgotten. They'll probably let the same thing happen all over again, and allow Germany to do whatever it wants until it gets out of control, and Europe can't handle it. Then of course they call on America to sort things out, and of course we go running every time. The rest of the world sees us now for the suckers we are, but we never learn. It's not our responsibility to sort out the messes other countries make for themselves.'

'Bob,' said Susan, 'if I were you, I'd take that food away right this minute and eat it, because if it gets cold and has to be heated up again, it probably isn't going to be worth eating.' Bob looked down at the pork and rice as if he'd never seen them before, and without another word, he left the kitchen.

'Your father never changes,' said Susan, opening a bottle of soy sauce, 'always talking and thinking about places and things far away, things that don't concern him.'

'He has a point,' Ted said mildly. I could imagine Bob saying exactly the same thing in the same way, in defence of Ted. 'After all, Mom, he was there, wasn't he? Remember all those things he told us about being in Germany at the end of the war? He's entitled to his opinion about what might happen in Europe, same as everybody else.'

But Susan couldn't understand why anyone would want to claim their right to an opinion on so boring a subject. 'I still don't see what it has to do with him. Even if America does get involved, nobody's going to ask him at his age to go back to Europe and fight the Germans, now are they? So why worry about it?'

When we'd finished eating, Susan cleared the table and tidied the kitchen before going off to watch television. Ted went out of the room too, and I was on my own when Bob came back with his tray, the cat at his heels. 'Time to fix Uncle Silas his dinner, now that everybody else has got theirs.' As Bob opened a tin of food the cat cried a little with anticipation, then silently set to wolfing it down, as soon as the plate was put before it. Bob and I vacantly watched Uncle Silas as he ate.

'Susan thinks I think I know it all,' Bob said suddenly, 'but I don't. I just know what I saw, and I know that we'd be crazy to let it happen again. Crazy.

'You see, I was there. I was in Germany at the end of the last war, and I can't forget it. I still feel guilty – not for anything I did,' he added hastily. 'I didn't do anything there to be ashamed of. But I still feel guilty about things I saw, and sometimes I think that's even worse.'

At that moment, Susan came back in, and Bob immediately changed the subject. 'Never saw a cat that loved its food as much as Uncle Silas. Maybe we'll give him a little bit more, eh? What do you say to that?' The cat started to mew again as Bob opened a second tin.

I thought life in America was so hard for people, and it didn't take me too long to work out the reason. America isn't a country, it's a continent. It's too big for people to live comfortably there, because it isn't on a human scale. The human body isn't designed to cope with the dimensions in which it finds itself there. Because the country is out of proportion to people, they try to make themselves feel safe by bringing things up to the same large scale. That was the only plausible reason I could think of for the size of everything, for the excess which amounted to so little: the vast fridges and freezers crammed to bursting point with jumbo-sized packets of food; the huge televisions with thirty-nine channels; fat newspapers with more supplements than you could ever be reasonably expected to read; the big cars in which people spent absurdly long periods of time going from place to place. I found all this enervating rather than comforting, and I think it has the same effect on most people. America isn't so much a country as a phenomenon.

On our last day in Washington, I stayed at home with Susan while Ted went into town to do some things. Susan and I had a good morning together. We made fudge brownies and drank coffee; she showed me all the things her new food processor could do, and I gave her some pasta recipes. It was pleasant and relaxed in a way that would have been impossible had I been with my own mother, but with Susan it was no problem because we both knew it was all a game. Without a word being said about it, we pretended that things were as they might have been twenty years ago. I was the nice girl who was going to marry Ted, and I'd be like a daughter to Susan. Ted and I would buy a house and have a couple of children and I'd make fudge brownies in my own kitchen and bring them over to her, and we'd swop household hints and go shopping together, and everything would be just dandy. And because we both knew there was never the slightest possibility of that happening, we could pretend for a while, and enjoy the illusion.

After lunch, which we made together, Susan brought out a box and poured a heap of old family photographs on to the kitchen table. We looked through them together. It was funny seeing pictures of Ted, because he's one of those people who remain completely recognizable throughout their lives. He looked himself in his baby photos, and if he lives to be ninety, he'll probably be just an older version of himself as he is now. It might almost go without saying that I'm not at all like that. I once showed Ted a photo of myself when I was a student, and not only did he not recognize me, he would hardly believe it when I told him it was me. I just changed as I grew up: you would never know *me* from my baby photos, but I have to admit that I've also worked a lot on changing my image and appearance at different periods in my life. You can do a lot with clothes and hairstyles and make-up if you know what you're about. There were photos of Ted sitting on the bonnet of an old 1950s car, Ted in a little baseball suit with a bat as big as himself, Ted sitting on the knee of an old lady – the 'Grammy' he had told me about the first time I went to visit him in Florence – Ted in his teens wearing a tuxedo, taking his girlfriend to a Prom.

Ted's sister Amy was in some of the photos, a happy little girl when she was small, but as she grew older her face became progressively more sullen and shut, until she was about twenty. There were no photos of her after that age. 'Amy's in Phoenix now. I'm not really sure what she's doing there: working in a hotel but I don't know exactly what she's doing. Bob and I had hoped she'd be able to come home for Thanksgiving last year, but she never came.'

Bob came into the kitchen to make a coffee while we were there, and he came over to the table to look at the photographs too. There was one of him in his army uniform, which he laughed at. 'Skinny little guy, wasn't I? Don't remember being so skinny!' Then he picked up a family group, and he laughed again. 'God, look at us, Susan! We look like Mr and Mrs America 1958, we look like we were advertising something.' Then Ted came back, and he groaned when he saw what we were doing. 'Mom, I can't believe you,' he said, but he was fascinated too, and began to look through the photographs with us. Bob took his coffee and two brownies back to his own room, and Ted, Susan and I went on looking at the old pictures together until Ted at last said, 'That's enough. Let's put all this away, it's making me feel ancient.'

15

Ted and I were to travel to New York by train, and Bob offered to drive us to Union Station. Susan made us a big packed lunch to eat on the train, even though Ted told her twice that it wasn't necessary, that we would be in New York long before lunch time. When I said goodbye to Susan she hugged me, but I could see that she expected never to see me again, and that it didn't bother her at all. She would forget me, she was starting to forget me even before I left. I wasn't the first woman she had seen Ted with, and I wouldn't be the last. If I had been foolish I would have been hurt or upset by this. Her attitude made me realize and admit to myself that Ted and I would go our separate ways sooner or later. Susan was only being realistic, not spiteful.

But when Bob said goodbye to me at the station, he had tears in his eyes. He also knew that he would probably never see me again, but it was as if he knew that the frailty of my relationship with Ted wasn't the only reason, that it also had something to do with Bob himself. It was as if he were going to his death, and it was that which was causing us to part, rather than that Ted and I were going to New York on a train. He looked so lonely, and suddenly I could see the emptiness of his life: a distant son, a hostile daughter, a wife with whom he had little in common. I pictured him in his room, alone, smoking, still trying to make sense of his memories of war. Maybe it was because he looked like Ted that I found it so sad. It was like meeting Ted years hence, and seeing that his life had been unhappy. We were bound to part but I would still care for him, and I hated to think that his life might end like his father's. I couldn't bear to watch Bob as he walked away from us.

I was a bit thrown by what had happened when I was saying goodbye: even though, as we sat on the train and I thought about it, nothing *had* really happened. Ted and I didn't talk about it: I wondered had he even noticed anything amiss. I looked at him from time to time as we went north, reading the *Washington Post*, occasionally glancing out of the smoked-glass windows of the train. Ted was inscrutable in the way good-natured people often are. I didn't know how he felt about leaving his parents, whether it bothered him or not. It was strange, because in some ways we were so close, and yet often I had no idea what was going on in his mind.

When I was a child, I was always getting into trouble for staring at people. Once a week, I used to go with my mother by bus to Ballyvaughan to do some shopping, and she always used to warn me before we left home to behave myself, and not gawp and gawk at people. I found it very hard to resist. When you're a child, strangers are completely fascinating. The world you move in is so familiar that things beyond it catch your imagination: pictures in books of foreign countries, and people you don't know. I used to look at the people on the bus, and I'd wonder about them. What was that woman in the tweed coat and flat shoes really like? If she was my mother, would she be good to me? Would she be like my mother and cook me turnips once a week, even though she knew I hated them? If that boy with the sports bag was my brother, would he have given me a kitten the way Jimmy did? Was that man as cross as he looked? If I was his daughter, what would he do to me? And then I would look back at my mother, and feel comforted, safe from any worries that might have been stirred up by my thoughts. I enjoyed the frisson of fear that came from imagining the woman across the aisle thrashing me with her shoe, or locking me in my room because I wouldn't eat my dinner, for I knew my own mother wouldn't do those things. It reassured me to look at her, because she was as familiar to me as my own fingers. I felt safe with my mother.

Imagining strangers as my parents was one thing. Imagining my parents as strangers was another. I began to play that game too, and I found that it was more dangerous than the other one. In the end, I couldn't handle it.

One day I was out in the car with my father. He was driving to the next village to collect a piece of farm machinery. I was on holiday from school, and he had asked if I wanted to go with him so I'd said yes. He didn't say anything as we drove along. My father didn't talk much at any time, and I often used to wonder what he was thinking. I prattled on to him for a bit, then I fell quiet. I started to do the same thing that I would do on the bus. I wiped from my mind all memory of my father, and pretended he lived in a different place, perhaps with another family, perhaps on his own. Maybe he wasn't a farmer but a lorry driver, or a man who owned a shop. I looked at his thick fingers gripping the steering wheel, and I wondered what he sold, groceries or hardware. I imagined him wearing an overall the colour of a brown paper bag, and people coming to him to buy hammers and nails and tins of paint. And then suddenly it wasn't make-believe any more: this man *was* a total stranger. I was terrified. 'Who is this person?' I thought. 'Where is he taking me? What will he do with me when he gets there?' I looked up at his face. His heavy brow was angry and cruel. 'Stop the car, please,' I said. He glanced over at me. 'What is it Aisling?' he asked. 'Don't you feel well?' but although he slowed down, he didn't stop. I still didn't trust this man. 'Stop the car!' I screamed, fumbling with the locks to get out, and this time he did, the brakes screeching. I already had the door of the car open, and the sight of the road moving beneath me frightened me so much, I let the door slip closed again, and started to cry.

Immediately the spell was broken, I knew he was my father, and I cried and cried, whingeing out between my tears, 'I'm sorry, Daddy, I'm sorry,' but I wouldn't tell him what I was sorry for. Of course he took me straight back home. I flung myself howling at my mother's skirts, and I said over and over silently to myself, 'This is my mother, this is my mother, she will look after me.' I gave my imagination no possible leeway. They thought I was sick and I let them; they wanted to put me to bed and I went. They brought me tea and toast later in the day, and although I was just at the stage when I was growing out of bears and soft toys, I spent the rest of the day with a teddy wedged firmly under my arm. When my mother brought me the toast, she tried to coax out of me what the problem was, but I only started to cry again, so she let the matter drop. The next morning, I was the first one up in the house, and I was resolutely cheerful. I didn't let anyone talk much about what had happened, and before long it was forgotten. But I didn't forget.

Now it was years since I had thought about that day, and sitting beside Ted on the train to New York, I realized that I was in danger of doing exactly the same thing again. If I thought about it too much, I would begin to wonder who this man beside me was, why on earth was I going to New York with him, what would happen to me when we got there? I struggled to distract myself from my own imagination. I asked him if there was anything interesting in the paper, and started to poke in the bag of food his mother had given us. Ted looked at me in amazement. 'You can't possibly be hungry already,' he said, as I pulled out apples and muffins, and of course I wasn't.

I looked out of the train window and asked him where we were. He said that he wasn't sure. It was the sort of journey where if you didn't bother to look out the window for a long time, you could be fairly sure that you weren't missing anything much. I pulled a doughnut apart and nibbled at it. The train stopped in Philadelphia, and I remember thinking that even by just looking at the city through a train window, you could tell that there was something missing. It reminded me of the area beyond S. Giorgio, where I worked. In Ireland I had seen little fields which had more psychic energy in them than you can sometimes find in whole cities. I could imagine hundreds of cities all over America which looked like this: activity, speed, emptiness; concrete, metal, glass, nothing. I wondered what it would be like to come from such a city, and then of course I glanced again at Ted. He had put on his Walkman: *The Magic Flute* was leaking out of the headphones. His eyes were closed, his face contented as a sleeping baby's. I saw then how foolish my line of thought was. As if all city people were inevitably alienated, and country people balanced and whole! I was the one who came from what looked like a rural idyll, and I was the one who was anxious and tormented. I was annoyed with myself for having fallen into this stupid notion, for I'd known for years that big cities didn't have the monopoly on evil, hate and unhappiness.

My first sensation as we approached New York was of claustrophobia. This feeling stayed with me and grew stronger the whole time we were there. The train disappeared into a tunnel, and we stayed underground until we arrived in Penn Station. Moments later, we were closed up in a taxi, and I really mean closed up. There was a thick, dirty perspex screen between us and the driver, with a cluster of little holes to speak through, and a hatch for money. The tight, closed space of the taxi contrasted strangely with the long high streets along which we sped. A short while later we were sitting in the dimmest and most cramped hotel room I'd ever seen. I felt a mounting sense of panic, which Ted didn't pick up on. He suggested that we rest a while before going out into the city and I readily agreed. We lay beside each other for an hour or so, and Ted fell asleep, but I didn't.

When he awoke, we went out for a walk. Every city has its own smell, and New York smells of concrete and iron. I thought it was strange to see the steam coming from the manholes in the road, pluming up in the cold air. In Central Park it was wintry, the ground yellow and hard, but the sun shone from a clear sky on the joggers in their shiny tight Lycra suits. I'd expected to see people jogging there, but I hadn't expected to see the stones, the huge bare rocks that broke the ground in Central Park. They surprised me because my image was of a completely artificial city, where every last vestige of nature had been obliterated. I had expected the park to be as featureless as a football pitch, and I was amazed to see these ancient rocks. Although they were in themselves completely unattractive, they delighted me simply by being there.

The following morning we had breakfast at a diner on Lexington Avenue which Ted knew from previous visits to New York. We sat up on high stools at the counter, and watched a man in a greasy white overall cook rapid breakfasts on a big hotplate. We took our time: watching him flip over rashers of bacon and pour eggs into metal rings was as important to me as the coffee and cinnamon toast I'd ordered. A waiter came over and apologized to the cook for some mistake he'd made. 'Sorry,' the waiter said, and the cook replied, 'Yeah, well don't be sorry, be careful.' We seemed to be the only people who weren't in a rush. Around us customers came and went, their food quickly ordered, quickly served, quickly eaten, and then they were gone. There was a big poster on the wall about what to do if someone chokes. I supposed they needed it because people ate so quickly there that they were probably quite likely to choke. I tried to keep my hands under the counter as much as possible, because they were shaking with nervousness, and I didn't want Ted to see that.

'I'm glad this place is still here,' he said. 'In Manhattan, you can never be sure: shops and restaurants are always folding. You go back to a place you knew and liked, and you find it's gone, it's as if it never existed.' What he said didn't surprise me. Already I had felt in the city that uneasy contrast of the solid and the evanescent. Even though it was a vast metropolis of metal and stone, you could smell the impermanence. Later in the day we saw the Trump Tower, a perfect name for a perfect example of this phenomenon. Outside it was a huge solid building; inside it was as vulgar and frail as a poor man's dream of riches. The crass pink marble walls with a fake waterfall running down them looked like they had been built yesterday, and would be dismantled again the day after tomorrow. I'd seen the same thing in reverse in S. Giorgio: on a summer morning when I drove down to the plain and looked back, the little town could seem like something in a dream. A cluster of creamy-coloured buildings girdled by a wall and wrapped in a pearly soft light, it was like a mirage: but those walls were two metres thick, and they had been there when Manhattan was a bare island with just a few ancient rocks sticking out of the soil.

A city acts on you like alcohol: it only brings out what is already there – sleepiness, laughter, violence – but it doesn't actually cause these things. New York brought out in me a deep anxiety, and a sense of distance from Ted. More unsettling, it brought out a sense of distance from myself. At night, looking out of the hotel windows at the water towers, the fire escapes, the tall buildings riddled with lit windows, where strangers moved, I began to feel a stranger to myself.

I went into the bathroom, locked the door and looked in the mirror. 'This is my face, my hair, my eyes, my self,' I said over and over again, and I conned the details of my own life to remind myself who I was. I tried to make myself believe in the reality of my own past, but it didn't work. On the middle finger of my right hand, I wear my mother's wedding ring. After she died Jimmy took the ring from her finger and gave it to me. I put it on, and I've never taken it off since then. It's the only thing I own that I really care for: all my other possessions mean nothing, they're like parts of a costume. When I left Paris, if I could have afforded it, I'd have thrown away every last thing I owned, gone to Italy in what I stood up in, and started there all over again. But looking now at my mother's ring in the hotel bathroom, I couldn't connect with it. Like seeing a ring on a stranger's hand in a public place, I knew it was charged with emotional significance: but not for me. I was indifferent to my own life, and yet I felt a sense of panic that this should be so. It frightened me to lose myself to myself in this way.

During the following days, this feeling didn't leave me, and to compensate I fixed my attention on the people I saw in the streets. The more distant their life and culture were from my own the more they fascinated me, like the Jewish diamond merchants on 47th Street, whom I saw on a raw dark evening, when I was waiting for Ted outside the Gotham Book Mart. In Chinatown, an old man sold tea eggs from a little wagon on the pavement. People were praying before a golden statue in a temple.

That sense of enclosure I had noticed as soon as I arrived in New York began to bear in on me. The city was like a cement trap. Standing on the intersection of West 57th Street and Madison Avenue, I looked right, left, behind and ahead of me, and saw in every direction long straight streets and towering buildings. I knew that beyond this there were more such streets, more such buildings, and I longed for space, but I knew that there was no escape. I was trapped in this massive, violent labyrinth.

One evening, when we were looking for a place to have a drink before dinner, Ted suddenly said, 'What about over there?' He pointed across the road to The Shamrock Inn, and I think he was a bit taken aback by the vehemence with which I said, 'No!' We found another bar.

'I didn't mean to be rude,' I said to him, when we'd sat down. 'It's just that fake Irishness is the last thing I could take now. I keep thinking of all the people I knew back in Clare who migrated. I know so well the place they left, and it's strange now to see where they came to.'

'It's the other way round for me,' Ted said. 'I still want to go and see the place in Sligo my grandfather came from.'

It was all so arbitrary. It could have been my grandfather who migrated. I could have been born in the States. If I had been born in a different place, at a different time, would I still be my self? 'I hope you get to see Ireland,' I said, looking intently at the glass in my hands. I'd never felt lonelier than when I was in New York.

I'd been lonely before, but this was different, and I couldn't understand it. I looked around the bar at all the other people sitting there, drinking, smoking, talking, laughing. I had a vague sense that the solution to what was tormenting me lay in the lives of strangers, but I couldn't get through to it. All I could set against this emptiness was the memory of home. I could go back, but it would be different now. I thought of Jimmy, of my father and mother, lost to me now, but they also had their part in what I needed to know. I had all the pieces, but I didn't know how to fit them together.

I drank three glasses of white wine, and when we went out into the street to look for a place for dinner, I suddenly threw my arms around Ted and kissed him. I was as surprised as he was: I'm not usually a demonstrative person, particularly in public places. It was so cold in the street that we decided to eat in the first affordable place we came to, which unfortunately turned out to be a phony Bavarian beer cellar called The Black Forest. A waitress wearing a dirndl, an apron and a badge saying, 'Hi, I'm Shirlee,' served us bratwurst and fries, and we wondered how many of the huge steins of beer you'd have to drink before you started thinking you were in Germany. Ted explained to me his theory that having a bad dinner in a tacky joint with someone you love is actually much more romantic than a conventionally romantic place with low lights, high prices and candles on the tables, where people just tend to get nervous. He had a point. We finished the night with apfel strudel, schnapps and a taxi back to the hotel.

The next morning, in the Metropolitan Museum, standing before a painting by Lucas Cranach, I felt oddly guilty. I'd never before seen a museum quite like the Met. Like the Museum of Air and Space in Washington, I felt it had palpable designs upon the people who visited it, but this time I succumbed completely, stunned by the size and the quality of the collections. I had gone there particularly to see the paintings, because painting is my first love, and I hadn't expected to be so interested in the other things, like the archaeological and ethnological collections, but they turned out to be unforgettable. Masks from West Africa, totems and sculptures from Papua New Guinea, Greek statues and Assyrian bas-reliefs: I went from one to another in complete fascination. It was like the city itself, a vast cultural mix, but here nothing was fake.

In the Met, there's an ancient Egyptian temple, small but whole, moved stone by stone to America and reconstructed there. It stands in a room with huge sloping windows, through which you can see the trees of Central Park, the skyscrapers and the sky. I sat for a long time before this juxtaposition of the very old and the contemporary, and I wondered what would happen to the temple eventually. It would probably be still there in a hundred years, maybe even another two hundred – but another five hundred? A thousand? To think of your own life ending is easy to imagine but hard to bear. To think of the end of the civilization in which you live is easy to bear, because it's hard to imagine. Life is so short, and it has its own pace and momentum. What you understand of it at any given time is always out of step with life itself – at least, that's how it is with me. I had a vague sense that during the preceding year my life had changed significantly, and the changes were not yet complete, but I couldn't understand what they were. I still lived and worked in the same place, and although I was fond of Ted, I knew it was only a matter of time until we drifted out of each other's lives. No, it was little things that gave me hints about a big change. I was on better terms with Jimmy than I had been a year previously. I felt lonelier more often than I used to. I thought more about my family and my childhood than in the past. I tried to avoid thinking about the future, but such questions pressed ever more urgently on my mind. Never mind what would have become of the temple in a thousand years, what would have become of *me* in five years' time?

Two Italian tourists sat down beside me, and I idly listened in to their conversation. The man was complaining that his feet were sore. Then they started to discuss where they would go for lunch, would they go back to the same place they'd been to yesterday, or would they try one of the places recommended in the book? It was nice just to listen to their voices and to remember Italy. I felt like I'd been away from it for such a long time. I've never got used to how, as soon as you go somewhere, it swamps out the place you've just left, no matter how vivid or important that place is to you. It may take a little time, but it always happens. A day or two later, I'd be back in Italy, a few more days and Italy would be overwhelmingly real, and America would be a memory. I couldn't believe it was just a few weeks since I'd been to Siena with Ted, and visited the gallery there. I remembered longing to go to America, to be in a place where the weight of history was absent. And now I knew I'd missed the point completely. I looked forward to returning.

16

The day after we got back from the States was *Carnevale*. When Franca called up to see how the trip had been, she brought with her a dish full of the special cake they make in Umbria for *Carnevale*, a type of fried batter made sticky with honey. Ted was still there when she called. He never ceased to be amazed at the number of celebratory dishes that Franca managed to come up with, it seemed that every time he was in S. Giorgio she was at the door with a plateful of something special for the *festa* of that particular day, and that she celebrated the unlikeliest festivals, such as the Feast of the Dead, with the most unexpected of dishes, such as chocolate cake made with pasta.

'I suppose this will be the end of the celebrations until Easter, Franca,' Ted said, lifting a cake from the plate and licking the honey from his fingers.

'Oh yes,' she replied. 'Except for Mother's Day, and then Women's Day.' She told us that Lucia was going to a *Carnevale* party that night, dressed as a rabbit. She had bought herself a set of ears and a fluffy tail, and had been experimenting with make-up for days, to try to perfect her nose and whiskers. Franca said that if we opened the shutters that gave on to the square, we would probably see the children from the elementary school coming out in their costumes later that morning. I opened the long glass balcony doors in the kitchen.

I had brought Franca a bottle of Californian wine from the States, and as soon as she saw it, she went into hysterics of laughter. I had known that the idea of Americans making wine would amuse her (but she was forced to admit, two days later, when she'd drunk it, that it had been very good). She wanted to know all about America: What had it been like being in a skyscraper? When you took a lift up to the hundred-and-first floor, did it feel like you'd left your tummy on the ground? Had I been attacked in New York? Had I seen anybody being attacked? What was the food like, was it as bad as everyone said? Did I get anything other than hamburgers to eat? Ted drank his coffee and ate his cake while he listened, half amused, and, I could see, half irritated. I wondered if perhaps Franca was laying it on a bit thick just to tease him, but it was quite possible that she was being serious. She'd never made any secret of the fact that she thought America was beyond the pale.

When we heard the children shouting in the square, we all went out on to the balcony. Below us, we could see a group of excited little bears and pirates and cavemen and devils, lobbing handfuls of confetti at each other and screaming. Their mothers had come to collect them from school, and we watched until the crowds thinned out, and then the square was empty, but for the paper confetti whirling and drifting in the light breeze that made the curtains billow into the room behind us. The kitchen was flooded with light. I always thought Italy was a lovely country to come back to. I was happy to be home.

Ted took the train back to Florence the following morning, and in the afternoon Franca called up to see me again. She had been in such good spirits the day before that I was a bit surprised to see how gloomy she was now. I knew, however, how moody she could be, and she never made any attempt to hide it. I offered her coffee, which she accepted, and we chatted over it in a scattered sort of way. Then, without any warning, she put her cup down, her face crumpled up like an unhappy child's and she began to cry, completely without restraint.

'They're going to cut me up, Aisling, and I'm so frightened, and it's not fair!'

'What is it, Franca?' I said. 'What's wrong?'

'I've got to go to the hospital,' she said through her tears, 'and they're going to cut me open here,' and she touched her breast, 'and maybe they're going to cut it off, and maybe I'm going to die,' and her voice broke again.

162

'How long have you known about this?' I asked gently after a few moments.

'There was a little lump. I felt it once when I was in the bath. I was afraid of what it might be.'

'But when was that?'

She looked at her hands and mumbled, 'Four years ago.' I didn't say anything.

'But it didn't go away and then Davide felt it, and he nagged me to go to the doctor, so at last I did, I went two days ago, and now I have to go to the hospital. What'll I do? I'm so frightened, Aisling. I don't want to die. What'll Davide do without me? And Lucia?'

I made all the comforting noises I could. I said that she didn't know for sure that it was malignant, and that soon she would know, and wasn't that better than to go through what she had gone through these past four years; and even if she did have to have a breast removed, she would still have her life, and all those other things that are so easy to say when it isn't your body and your life that's under discussion and threat.

'It isn't fair,' she sniffed, digging the heels of her hands into her eye sockets. 'They took my womb away after Lucia was born. There'll be nothing left to know I'm a woman. I don't want to live all cut up, I don't want to be left as just a few bits and pieces.'

I asked her when she was going into hospital, and she said, 'Tomorrow.' I promised that I would go to see her, and she was happy about that.

After she had gone back down to her own apartment, I went out on to the balcony, and looked down into the square. It was a bright day, and I felt that odd sense of dislocation that comes when you've just heard something really shocking, and then you look at something mundane, the sun, trees, people in the street, and you can't reconcile them at all. If this terrible news is true, can ordinary things still happen, still exist? Can Franca have cancer and the sun still shine? People still cross the square, coming from her very own shop with bags of groceries and loaves of bread? People still squabble and shout in the bars? If I was the one who was ill, could it all possibly go on? Of course it could. Of course.

You can get used to anything. In a day or two I accepted and believed in the reality of Franca's situation, and its simultaneous existence with the sun, the people in the bars and shops, with the life that was going on blankly around us. Things unfolded as if pre-ordained. Franca went into hospital; she had cancer; they removed her breast. She cried and sobbed and railed against it, and then she came home from hospital and lay in bed, crying and sobbing there, while Davide and Lucia did their best to humour and distract her. It was very hard for Davide, because he had to bear the brunt of her obsession. Franca was convinced that she was mutilated and ugly. She wouldn't believe Davide when he said that it didn't make any difference to him, and that he still loved her, but Franca said that that was all lies. It was as if she wanted him to reject her, so that then she could say, 'You see, I was right. I knew you'd love me less because of this.'

One night Lucia called up to see me. She looked tired and drawn. She was doing a lot of extra work in the shop, to make up for Franca's not being there, and of course she was worried and upset about what was happening in the family.

'Poor Papa,' she said. 'Mama's always watching him to see if he's looking at other women. He doesn't, but she won't believe him. When there are women on television with big chests she takes it personally, as if it was intended to annoy her, and she gets really angry if she thinks Papa's looking at them. And it's hard, Aisling, because the problem is this: so many of the women on television are big, and they wear hardly any clothes, even the ones advertising things like margarine. I never noticed that until now. Poor Papa. He's looking forward to the World Cup, he should be able to watch that without Mama getting too upset.'

'You're doing a good job, Lucia.'

'It is very hard, Aisling. I'm so worried about Mama. I don't know what Papa and I would do without her. Did you look after your mother when she was sick?'

I said no, that my mother had fallen ill when I was away, and that she was only ill for a day or so before she died. I was a bit caught off guard by Lucia asking me this, because during the time of Franca's illness I often thought about it. When I went down to their apartment and Lucia was patiently nursing her mother, or just keeping her company, I used to think of how it hadn't been like that for me with my own mother. Deep down, I did feel guilty in that empty, futile way one feels about things that are long past and irrevocable. Most absurd of all, I knew that if I had my life to live over I'd do exactly the same thing again: but I still felt guilty.

Franca gradually got over her operation, as the spring wore on. She was too inquisitive to stay completely out of circulation for a long time, although she still refused to go back to work in the shop. 'How could I face people?' she'd say. Davide tried to encourage her, pretending that he could hardly cope without her, but she said that he would have to get used to it. 'Nobody's indispensable,' she said. 'What if I die? You'll have to manage without me then, won't you? And I might die, nobody ever said I wouldn't.' She did spend a lot of time in the shop between one o'clock and half past four when the shutters were down, checking the money, rearranging the shelves, sorting things out and ordering stock.

What she said was true, but morbid, and no help or consolation to Lucia or Davide. As time went on, I suppose I began to feel less sorry for her. I thought she was wallowing in her grief, and I commented on this to Ted on the phone one night, of how her constantly looking on the black side was getting on my nerves a bit. I was taken aback when he said sharply, 'Well, now you know what it's like to be on the receiving end.' I didn't know how to answer that.

Franca went back to the hospital for check-ups quite often, and would have to continue to do so for quite some time. She never fought her illness, but lay down under it from the first. When she was feeling particularly sorry for herself (which was often) she said that she knew she was going to die, that there was nothing ahead of her but a slow, painful death, which had already begun. I didn't always take her seriously. I had more sympathy for her family than I did for her. Franca was always so sorry for herself that I felt an extra ration of pity was the very last thing she needed.

It was a beautiful spring: if anything, too beautiful, for it became warm very early, and hardly rained at all. The weather was to continue like this, all the way through to the summer. Easter came around. 'It doesn't mean as much as it used to,' Franca said, and this time she spoke out of something other than unmitigated gloom. 'Easter means less now, because Lent means nothing. Every day of the year now, people have cakes and sweets and nice things to eat, and plenty of them. Time was when things were different. I remember when I was small, growing up on the farm. For weeks you'd be praying and eating simple food, and then on Easter Sunday, there'd be such a lunch! I suppose we weren't supposed to eat a lot in Lent as a form of penance, but for me it only made the feast at the end taste twice as good. The children now don't know what it is not to have all the things they want, and to have them right now.'

It was late at night on the Monday of Holy Week, and Franca and I were standing in her shop. I'd been on my way upstairs, and she'd called to me to come through for a moment and talk to her. She was surrounded by chocolate bells, and chocolate eggs wrapped in vast flourishes of coloured foil. I asked her how business was, and she said that things were going well. 'I'll make you a proper Easter cake, Aisling,' she said. With her toe she poked at a box with a picture on it of a cake in the shape of a dove. 'None of this rubbish that just comes out of some factory up in Milan. I'll be making cheese pizza and sweet cake, and I'll give you some of both. Get you a bottle of *vernaccia* too, if you want.' In spite of herself, Franca was eagerly looking forward to Easter. In a closely observed round of feasts and festivals and customs, for her, Easter was the most important, surpassing even Christmas, about which she thought far too much fuss was made. Had she been well, she'd have gone to Mass on Easter Sunday morning, but more from tradition than belief. She didn't make any connection between a festival centred on death and resurrection and her own situation. Resurrection in particular didn't impress her.

'It's not that I don't believe it,' she said. 'It's more that I don't understand it, and what I don't understand I never have much use for. Even if it does happen, it won't be for a long time, and even then, it just won't be the same. The thing is, Aisling, I just love life. It's as simple as that. I know it's full of problems, and I moan about it just as much as anybody else, but I can't see a way to improve it. When we were children, we used to try to think of improvements you could make to the human body. We thought of so many things, but there was always a catch. We decided in the end that maybe people's bodies weren't perfect, but they were the best you could imagine. I feel the same way about life.

'When I was small, I had this book, too, where I used to read all these stories about fairies and Princes and Princesses, and there was always a lot about jewels and riches. There was one story I always remember, about a Princess who had a pair of golden slippers, encrusted with diamonds and emeralds and rubies. I thought that they must be the most wonderful things; I used to dream about having a pair of shoes made of gold. Of all the stories, that was the one I liked best. And then I grew up and I thought about it, and I thought it was the most foolish thing in the world. How could anyone ever wear a pair of solid gold slippers? Can you imagine anything more painful? Golden slippers are useless, Aisling. There's nothing better than ordinary life, and if I've learnt anything from my time on this earth, it's that, and I want to keep living.

'Yesterday I was in my room, and it was almost lunchtime. My mother-in-law was cooking in the kitchen, Lucia was just in from school. I could smell the sauce for the pasta, and then your car pulled up outside, same as that time every day. I heard the car door close and you said hello to Davide, and then I heard the crash of him pulling down the shutters of the shop. I thought, "This is what death means: all these things will still be going on, but I won't be here any more." And I thought my heart would break.'

Ted was coming to stay with me at Easter. Franca invited us both to have Easter Sunday lunch with the family, and Davide came up to my apartment to plead with me to accept. I'd hesitated because I didn't want to give them extra work, but he thought that cheerful company was just what she needed. He said that it would be good for her to spend some time with people from outside the family. She seemed very fond of my *amico americano*, and whatever made Franca happy would please the whole family.

And so Ted and I had Easter lunch with Franca and the others, and everybody enjoyed it. A ham had been sent down from the farm in the hills: meat from the pig we had seen being butchered at New Year. Franca set it up in a big metal frame which held it tightly, then she cut paper-thin slices from it. The delicate flavour of the ham was much commented on. Franca had a great time, teasing Ted, heaping his plate with roast lamb, and explaining how everything was made. She had an unfortunate habit of cramming her mouth with food just before starting to tell him how a particular dish was cooked, with the result that he couldn't understand a word she was saying. She made him drink lots of *vernaccia*, and at the end of the meal, a large chocolate egg was cracked open with great ceremony.

Later that afternoon, Ted and I drove up into the hills, parked, and went for a walk. After a while we sat down under some olive trees, and looked down at S. Giorgio, neatly girdled by its walls, and the hazy plain far below.

'On a day like this,' I said, 'I know why I'm still living in S. Giorgio.' In Umbria, the dreamy round of the seasons, the festivals, of life itself was so complete that once you had stepped into that charmed circle, it was almost impossible to pull yourself away again. Franca would have asked why anyone would ever want to leave such pleasures, but for me there was something missing. What was it? A sort of wildness. 'Sometimes,' I said to Ted, 'I'm afraid that it's all like a dream, and that someday I'll wake up, and feel that I've let so much of my life slip by, and with it something important, that I was too drowsy and wrapped in luxury to miss until it was too late. It's like living in a walled garden here – a fabulous garden, and one so big that you can't see the walls, but you know they're there, all the same. And yet on a day like this, none of that matters.'

I was glad that the winter was over, and I was even looking forward to the hot days of summer. I promised myself that this year I wouldn't complain but enjoy to the full the different atmosphere that falls over the country with the heat. It would be good to come home from work in the middle of a baking hot day, when the whole village would be stunned into silence. I'd have a light lunch: tomatoes, peaches, thing like that. Then with all the shutters still closed, I'd lie down to drowse and snooze for an hour under a cool white sheet, and I'd look at the light of the sun, coming through the slats of the shutter, and falling in long, broken lines on the bedroom ceiling. I'd listen to voices in the square: things even sound different in extreme heat, the way extreme cold throws a silence over the world.

In early May, Jimmy rang me to say that Nuala had given birth to a little girl. They were both delighted, and I was pleased for them too, and glad to hear the news. (I have to confess that I was completely indifferent to the births of both Sinead and Michael.) I don't really know why I felt so differently this time, but I do know that I was happy throughout that spring, between the time when I returned from the States, and what was to happen at the start of the summer. I was happy with Ted, and I thought I was close to Franca. Now I can see that I didn't understand her at all. Sometimes when I think of Franca, I think of what Pirandello said about Italians, how they are weeping behind a mask that laughs. No, I didn't understand Franca. I didn't see, didn't want to see, the extent of her melancholy. The strongest sun casts the blackest shadow. I didn't take her seriously. It's an age-old mistake. Other nationalities haven't been taking Italy seriously for years, they see a sort of buffoonery that isn't really there. I dismissed Franca's worries as histrionics, as part of a national tendency to over-dramatize things. Now I know I was wrong.

One day in May, Franca called up to see me again. She had bad news. The operation had failed to check the illness. She was going to have to go for extra treatment. She didn't believe that it was going to help her and, to be honest, by that stage, neither did I. This time I didn't wheel out any well-worn platitudes to her. I don't remember saying anything much that day, we just sat with our arms around each other for a while, and she rested her head on my shoulder. After she'd gone down to her own apartment, I went out on to the balcony: not the one which overlooked the square, but the bedroom balcony, which gave on to the back yard. I looked down at the two broken-down cars, the faded houses, the heap of old wooden crates. In the long grass of the overgrown garden, a cat was sitting washing its face. I remember thinking of what Franca had said to me before Easter, and I thought: 'She's right. Life is very precious.'

I don't remember if I was dreaming that morning: I probably was, I usually do. If I wake slowly I remember my dreams, but they get completely wiped out if I'm woken abruptly, for example, by an alarm clock going off, or, as was the case on this particular morning, by someone hammering with their fists on the door of my apartment, and shouting my name. It was Lucia. She was sobbing so much that I couldn't understand what she was saying, except that it concerned 'Mamma'. That much I had guessed. Opposite the main door of my apartment was another door, which opened on to a short flight of steps, leading to the attic. Usually this door was locked, but now it lay ajar, and Lucia, still crying, dragged me through it.

What I saw when we entered the attic shocked me so much, because, not in spite of, its being so familiar. The woman's hanging body, the stillness of it, the heaviness: I felt that same sense of constriction and of terror that I had known for months, when just this image haunted my mind. As Lucia threw her arms around me and wept, I knew that it would haunt her now too, more than I could ever imagine.

It was all over the papers the next day, and all over the billboards of the local papers outside the newsagents. The Italian press – and Italian society – take a very different attitude to privacy, compared to what I had grown up with, which probably went too far in the other direction. However, I still felt uneasy at the openness and insouciance with which such things were reported there. Only a few days earlier I had read about a man who had thrown himself off a bridge somewhere in Tuscany. He was on the bridge for six hours before he killed himself, and the paper reported, complete with photographs, how his wife had stood below pleading with him not to do it, holding little Lamberto by the hand, and little Roberta in her arms. It was enough for someone to be killed in a fire in a house for the by-line to run 'Suicide?'

There was some comfort in knowing that Franca would not have minded in the least having the details of her death all over the paper; in fact she would probably have been quite pleased. I had often seen her read similar cases with relish, down to the last morbid detail. She had said to me once, after telling me a particularly sensational piece of local gossip, 'You should never try to hide anything, Aisling. If you have a secret, it's best to tell it to everybody as soon as you can, because they'll only find out about it anyway, and then it'll be twice as embarrassing.' Time and time again she trumped the aces of people who would have talked about her, and so she would probably have been very pleased with the local press for disseminating full details of the circumstances of her death: that she was a shop-keeper, that she had cancer but killed herself because she couldn't face the long-drawn-out illness, knowing that she was going to die at the end of it. She had thought that it would be better for the family, easier for them like this.

Which, of course, it wasn't. Davide was inconsolable, and stricken with guilt. In the week before she died, Franca had wanted to sleep in another room. She was often restless at night, and she told Davide that it would be better for him to get a decent night's sleep, as he had to work in the shop. 'I told her it didn't matter, Aisling,' he said to me, again and again, and to anyone else who would listen. 'I told her I'd rather she stayed with me, so that if she was sick or needed anything, I could get it for her, but she said no, and insisted on sleeping in the spare room.' And it was because she was there that she had been able to sneak up to the attic unheard in the small hours, and end her life. 'I'll never forgive myself,' Davide said.

The funeral was hastily arranged, and took place a day later. Even though I had been in Italy for a long time, it was the first funeral I had been to there, whereas when I was living in Ireland

I seemed to be going to them all the time. Franca's funeral struck me as a rushed, unnatural affair, lacking the Irish talent for mourning. You could see that everyone wanted it to be over as quickly as possible. This was in spite of Franca being in a massive, ornately carved coffin, which was placed in a hearse with gold trimmings on the roof. She couldn't have had more elaborate floral tributes, not if she'd been an Unknown Soldier on Remembrance Day. Don Antonio mumbled his way through the funeral Mass. There were lots of people there whom I recognized, including Michele and Patrizia from the farm, where we'd gone in January. Ted came down from Florence for the day. I found it hard to associate Franca with her own funeral, knowing how she always went her own way, no matter what the Church said. She had certainly gone her own way in death. It didn't matter to her that the Church said it was a sin of despair to take your own life: Franca had gone right ahead and done it.

Only afterwards, when we went to the high-walled cemetery did I feel some essence of Franca's self, her personality. I remembered being there with her on the Day of the Dead, and how carefully she had arranged the flowers she had brought with her, and lit the fat red candle. Spiritual things didn't interest her, but practical things did, and she had tidied the tomb as deftly as she set a table. I had known when Mass was being said that day that her mind was wandering all over the place, that she was thinking about lunch, about how cold she was, about the flowers the women beside her had brought: anything but death. They slotted her coffin into a long space like the top shelf of a cupboard, as if she were being put away for a few months, like a winter coat, instead of for always. Then we all went home.

I rang Ted every single night that week, and then on the Sunday night, just as he was about to ring off, I said, 'Wait, wait, I have something to ask you. I'm going back to Ireland for a few weeks in June. Do you think you'd like to come with me?'

17

'Well,' Nuala said to me, 'how does it feel to be home?'

'Good,' I lied. 'I'm glad to be back.' Truth was, sitting in Nuala's gleaming new kitchen I didn't yet feel that I was home. Nuala and Jimmy weren't exactly as I'd remembered or imagined them, and I realized this the moment Ted and I pushed our luggage trolleys out through customs at Dublin Airport, and saw Jimmy waiting for us. He had more of a middle-class gloss to him than before: smart grey slacks and a bottle-green v-necked pullover with the crest of a golf club embroidered on it. Golf! Jimmy had always been a mad-keen hurler. It was hard to imagine him sedately tapping a little white ball around a putting green. He looked older too: his hair had gone a bit grey at the temples, and I could see that he was quite nervous at meeting me again. That made me sad; but still, it was a much happier homecoming than my last visit to Ireland. Nobody spoke of it, but I know Jimmy was also thinking about the time our mother died. He'd also met me at the airport then. He'd been dressed in his best suit, and I knew to look at him that he'd been crying. That had shocked me. I'd never seen Jimmy cry before.

My life had been such a mess at that period. I had been in Italy just long enough to feel that moving there had been a big mistake, and I was tormented with guilt because my mother had asked me to go home and visit her, and I had refused, and now she was dead. Jimmy had reproached me bitterly for being away when she died, and I had felt my position indefensible (which hadn't stopped me from vehemently defending it). There'd been a lot of bad feeling between us when I left to go back to Italy a few days after the funeral, and I hadn't been back to Ireland since then.

Sinead and Michael had grown out of all recognition. Michael had been a baby, five years ago. Sinead said she remembered the last time I was in Ireland, but I wasn't convinced. Jimmy was right: she looked at lot like Nuala, but in terms of her character, I couldn't see that she was like me. She was far more sparky and confident than I remember being when I was ten. And now there was the new baby: and the new house. I tried not to smile when Sinead said guilelessly, 'Mammy says we used to live in a housing estate, but now we live in a development.' When Jimmy and Nuala got married, they bought a flat-fronted brick and plaster semi, with a fenced-in front garden. Their new place was far more up-market, with bay windows and a neat porch with a pointed roof. Each house had its own separate garden at the back, but at the front there were no divisions. Nuala proudly showed Ted and me around all the house. You could still smell the paint and the plaster. They hadn't yet furnished and decorated all the rooms: Nuala said they would do it slowly, as they could afford it, and so have everything just the way they wanted it. There was a microwave oven in the stripped pine kitchen. Things began to fit together for me. Now I could understand Jimmy's new slacks and golf-club sweater. I could understand why he was going grey too.

Bringing Ted to Dublin with me turned out to be a far smarter move than I'd realized it would be. Ever since leaving home to go to university, I'd kept my private life completely private from my family. To this day, Jimmy and Nuala don't know what happened in Paris. For years there was nobody in my life, but they didn't know that, and I think Nuala's imagination ran riot. If I was so secretive, there must have been something to hide. Like a lot of people whose emotional lives have followed a conventionally mapped-out route, she thought the only alternative to her way of doing things was heartless promiscuity. My own experience was of a messy, painful but sincere search for affection, where the ultimate goal wasn't a mortgage and a cast-iron marriage contract. Nuala wouldn't have been able to understand that at all. She never understood me: or, to be fair, we never understood each other. I probably didn't make much effort. She thought me strange because there's so little evident family feeling in me.

When I rang Jimmy to say that I'd be coming to Ireland with an American friend, he said at once that Ted would be more than welcome. Jimmy and Nuala took my telling them about Ted and bringing him home as a rare sign of trust and openness on my part. They were both very nervous when they met him – God knows what sort of man they expected to love me – but within half an hour Ted had completely won them over. Nuala really liked him, and that made it easier for her to get on with me.

Everything was so different on this visit that it didn't feel like I was at home. On the evening of the day we arrived, the four of us sat at the kitchen table over a Tea Time Express chocolate cake, and a pot of tea. 'Was Rome packed with people over for the World Cup?' Jimmy asked.

'There were quite a few,' I said, 'but not as many as I expected.' Ted told them about how we'd seen the children steal a wallet from a woman's bag the day before we flew to Dublin. Nuala shuddered. 'The stories you hear! They say people go about on motorbikes grabbing handbags from women there. I think I'd be too frightened to go to Rome.'

While I was still in Italy, I'd told Jimmy and Nuala a bit about what I planned to do when I was in Ireland. They knew that the following day we were going to collect a hire car, and drive over to Clare. They'd assumed that Ted was going to stay there with me, but I told them now that Ted had plans of his own: he was going to drive up to Sligo to see where his great-grandfather came from, and try to trace his roots. I promised Jimmy and Nuala that when we came back up to Dublin, we'd spend a few days with them before flying back to Italy. They seemed really pleased about that, and I didn't say it out of duty or politeness: it was something I wanted to do.

When we left Dublin the following morning, it was raining a bit, but I didn't care. We stopped on the way and bought some groceries, including matches and firelighters. Nuala had warned me to be sure to light a big fire, as soon as we arrived. Because of the new baby and moving house, they hadn't gone down there for a long time, and she said that the house would need to be well aired.

It was a good journey. Even when the scenery wasn't anything special, it was nice to see the lush greenness of the countryside, after the summer-scorched Italian landscape. Driving through the Bog of Allen, a large flock of starlings suddenly swooped low past us. Because the land was so flat and the sky so big and the birds so close, Ted said that he felt like he was flying, rather than travelling by car. Beyond Athlone, we saw the start of the sky that I consider to be my sky, with the big high clouds coming in off the Atlantic. I was glad to be going home, but I was nervous too. I didn't know what to expect, didn't know how I'd react to being there again. When at last I caught sight of the roof of the house in the distance, I didn't say anything to Ted.

I'd expected the house to look smaller than I remembered it, but I was taken aback at how shabby and run-down it was when we pulled up outside. The paintwork – light blue with dark blue door and windowframes – was badly weathered, and the little front garden that my mother had always kept so neat had gone completely wild. The currant and gooseberry bushes were choked with bindweed. While Ted got the luggage out of the boot, I cupped my hands around my eyes, and peered through the windows. I could see dim, familiar outlines, but it wasn't enough to prepare me for the moment I opened the front door and went inside.

It was as if I were shrinking, and all my spurious sophistication fell away. My elegance, my smart Italian shoes: all this counted for nothing now. The memories flooded in with such violence that the self I'd made since leaving home was wiped out, and when I turned and saw a man dragging a suitcase into the room I looked at him blankly, wondering for a moment who on earth he could be.

We lit a fire in the hearth, and I draped sheets over a chair before it, to air them. The chair had a limp cushion on it, with a crocheted cover in lots of different colours. I remembered my mother making it, out of scraps of wool. In the evening, I made dinner: potatoes, carrots and chops, and after it we had mugs of hot sweet tea, and I opened a packet of chocolate biscuits. It was raining hard. When I thought of Italy, it hardly seemed real to me. I couldn't believe that I'd left an apartment there full of things, clothes and books and records. I couldn't believe that my life was there. I looked at my watch, and tried to imagine the hot square, the people coming out of Davide's shop with baskets full of vegetables and bread, the coloured plastic tapes that hung in the doorway draping themselves over their shoulders. I could picture the scene, but it didn't have the reality of the thick striped mug in my hand. I poured more tea, and as I added milk, I thought of how Franca would have set her teeth in disgust.

Ted set off for Sligo the following morning. I'd helped him plan his route on a map the night before, and he was excited as a child. I told him to enjoy himself, and that I'd see him in a week's time.

I wasn't lonely when he went away. I realized then how much I'd needed that week on my own. I slept in my old room, with the table where I'd studied so hard for my Inter-Cert, longing to be away. My mother's old bike was in the shed. Jimmy had told me it was still in good shape, so I pumped up the tyres and went cycling to the village to buy food. I had no friends left locally, for I'd long since lost contact with everybody I'd known when I lived there, but in the village shop, everybody recognized me. I didn't feel comfortable, waiting to be served. People were friendly enough, probably on Jimmy's account. They all asked after him, and wanted to know about the new baby, was it a boy or a girl? But I felt they were sizing me up, and I felt judged for having been away when my mother died. My earliest memory is of being in the shop with her. She was wearing a white dress with red flowers on it, and an old lady was offering me a tube of Silvermints. I didn't want to take them, because the hand that held them out to me was so wrinkled and withered. I must have been barely three. All I can remember now are the sweets, the hand, and my mother's dress: it was one of those things that are just on the very edge of your life, so near to your not being capable of memory, so near to your not being there at all. I was older now than my mother was when I was born.

Every afternoon, I went for a walk, usually along the beach. After Umbria, the salt air and the crashing waves were marvellous. One day, on a flat rock, I found a little group of treasures all set out: a piece of green glass, rubbed smooth by the sea, a fragment of pottery, some shells, a curious stone. I thought of the child who must have found and put them there with such care, and how, later that day, when the tide came in, they would all be washed away, back into the Atlantic.

I did a lot of tidying and cleaning; and I threw a lot of things away, mainly clothes and old letters and papers. In the bottom of a drawer I even found the paper fan Yuriko had given me. It looked faded and tawdry, and I suppose I should have thrown it away too, but I couldn't bring myself to do it.

In the evenings, I cooked myself a simple dinner, and then sat by the fire reading until the small hours of the morning. I'd decided to re-read *The Idiot* while I was at home, and this time I understood why I liked it so much.

Ted phoned me one night in the middle of the week, from a payphone in a pub in Ballisodare. It was hard to hear what he was saying: one of the World Cup matches was on television, and there was a terrible racket, but he bawled down the line that he was having a great time. 'I think I've found a brother of my great-grandfather on a parish register here,' he shouted. He told me he'd see me in a few days, and he ran out of change while I was talking to him, so that I was left standing in the hall with the receiver buzzing.

The night before Ted was due back, I cycled out at dusk to 'he foot of one of the Green Roads. I left the bike there: the ground was too rough, and the hill too steep, and I wanted to walk, in any case. I like these overgrown roads you get in Clare, they're called the Green Roads or the Hunger Roads, and they lead to ruined villages which were abandoned during the Famine. I was fascinated by them when I was a child. If we had lived in the same place, but a hundred years earlier, I used to think, there wouldn't have been enough for my parents and Jimmy and me to eat. We would have had to leave our house, and go to America on a boat, and not just us, but everybody in our village would have gone, so that there'd have been nobody left behind to look after anything. And then, years and years later, we might have come back and looked for our home, but it would have been so ruined and tumbledown that we might not even have recognized it. It would be the saddest thing, I thought. But now I realized that what I had thought so awful had actually happened: our family home was empty and abandoned.

I walked on up to the brow of the hill. It was a beautiful still evening. The sky was a deep, radiant blue, and out over the sea there was a new moon. I came to the ruined village. The doorways and windows of the houses were packed with nettles, and small trees grew in the former rooms. I remembered reading somewhere that the Colosseum in Rome had been abandoned and untended right up until the end of the last century. By that time there were over four hundred species of plants growing there. Some of them weren't even native to Europe, having grown from seeds in the fodder of exotic animals brought to Rome to be killed in the games: lions, elephants, giraffes. Then, in a fit of late-nineteenth-century tidy-mindedness, the whole Colosseum was cleared out. Now fewer than thirty different types of plants grow there.

On a drystone wall near by, I suddenly noticed a large cat, silent, angular, blinking, and I wondered what advantage there was for a cat to be on a Green Road, late on a summer night. There must have been something to be gained, or else the cat wouldn't have been there. It looked at me coldly, and I moved away, for I didn't see any need to disturb it. I walked on a bit further, and sat down on a broken stone. A corn-crake was calling. I hadn't heard a corn-crake for years. Ted would be back the next day, and I thought of the places I would show him. I knew of a field where there was a well and a cross. A hazel tree grew over the well, and on the cross was a woman's head with a long pigtail. It had been weathered over the years: the pale stone had the texture of bread. It was a tiny field. There were high hedges all around, and it had the air of an ancient place. I knew

Ted would like it. I'd show him the Green Roads too, and Poulnabrone Dolmen, and we'd look for Bee Orchids. It might have been the other way round. My ancestors might have migrated, so that I would have been born in America, and come back looking for my roots. I watched the light bleed slowly out of the sky in a long, midsummer dusk, while the moon brightened. Then I thought of Italy, and at once the decision came into my mind, clear and resolute in a way it would never have been had I mulled over the question for weeks. I would leave S. Giorgio. When I went back to Italy, I would stay only as long as was necessary to pack my things, and work my notice in the factory. I'd come back here. I'd have to talk to Jimmy about it when we went back to Dublin, and I'd tell Ted what I was planning as soon as I saw him. I realized that he wouldn't be surprised.

I looked at my watch. It was later than I thought, so I turned and walked back on the grassy road. The corn-crake was still hoarsely calling, but the cat on the wall had gone.